"Thanks for bringing me here. For...for being there."

"It's okay. Of course I would bring you. And as for staying..." Nick shrugged. He didn't quite know what to think of his fierce desire to protect Beth that had less to do with Jim's request than his own need to be at her side.

"It meant a lot," Beth said quietly, her eyes holding his.

Nick felt an urge to touch her. To connect with her. His hand twitched at his side and as he lifted it the doors to the NICU swished open. Reality intruded into the moment in the form of Beth's mother-in-law, Ellen.

Ellen glanced at Nick and he got the hint that she wanted to be alone with Beth for a moment.

"I'll be waiting in the lobby," he said to Ellen. Then he glanced at Beth. "Congratulations, Beth."

But as he walked away, he wished he could stay.

He dismissed the thought. He wasn't Beth's husband and he had no right to be at her side.

In spite of his growing feelings toward her.

Books by Carolyne Aarsen

Love Inspired

A Bride at Last
The Cowboy's Bride
*A Family-Style Christmas
*A Mother at Heart
*A Family at Last
A Hero for Kelsey
Twin Blessings
Toward Home
Love Is Patient
A Heart's Refuge
Brought Together by Baby
A Silence in the Heart
Any Man of Mine
Yuletide Homecoming
Finally a Family
A Family for Luke
The Matchmaking Pact
Close to Home
Cattleman's Courtship
Cowboy Daddy
The Baby Promise

*Stealing Home

CAROLYNE AARSEN

and her husband, Richard, live on a small ranch in northern Alberta, where they have raised four children and numerous foster children and are still raising cattle. Carolyne crafts her stories in an office with a large west-facing window through which she can watch the changing seasons while struggling to make her words obey.

The Baby Promise
Carolyne Aarsen

Steeple
Hill®

Published by Steeple Hill Books™

STEEPLE HILL BOOKS

Steeple
Hill®

ISBN-13: 978-0-373-81522-7

THE BABY PROMISE

Copyright © 2011 by Carolyne Aarsen

Printed in U.S.A.

I lift up my eyes to the hills—
where does my help come from?
My help comes from the LORD,
the Maker of heaven and earth.
—Psalms 121: 1–2

I'd like to dedicate this book to all our soldiers serving overseas both in the battlefield and in peace-keeping missions. We may never know the extent of your sacrifice but we hope that you understand our appreciation of your dedication and heroism.

Acknowledgments

I'd like to thank Nita Rudmik for all her help with the neonatal questions.

I'd also like to thank Janelle and Mark Schneider both for the sacrifices they have made respectively as a soldier and wife of a soldier and for the information they gave me about the troops in Afghanistan. I only used the tiniest part of all they gave me and any mistakes or misrepresentation is mine and mine alone.

Chapter One

He wasn't supposed to be here, Nick Colter thought, his eyes looking over the log house nestled in a copse of pine trees, smoke curling out of the stone chimney.

The utter peace of the place eased away memories of dust, pain, brokenness and war, but behind that came the guilt.

"Can I help you?"

A melodic voice broke the quiet of the winter morning and Nick spun around, his hand reaching for the rifle he no longer carried.

He caught himself and flexed his tightening fingers, forcing himself to relax as he watched the petite woman walking toward him through the pine trees dusted with snow. These were the friendly mountains of Cochrane, Alberta, not the mountains of Afghanistan.

He wasn't a soldier anymore and the woman with the curly blond hair pulled loosely back from a heart-shaped face, cheeks rosy from the cold, wasn't an enemy.

"Sorry to startle you," she said as she walked toward him, choosing her steps carefully on the snow-packed driveway. "I just saw the cab leave."

"Yeah, I just got here." Nick poked his thumb over his shoulder at the car that was spinning out of the driveway, struggling to gain traction on the snow. He dropped his duffel on the ground as he watched the young woman come closer to him. She wore a pale blue woolen jacket straining over a rounded belly and black pants tucked into leather boots. In spite of the cold, she wore nothing on her head and her bare hands clutched the handle of a large black briefcase.

Beth Carruthers. Jim's widow. Looking even more beautiful than she did in the pictures his soldier buddy had shown him.

And pregnant with the child his friend had talked about so often and now would never see.

Nick walked toward her, pulling off his hat as he did. She stopped a few feet away from him, her expression guarded and cautious, her violet eyes narrowed.

"Hello, Beth. I don't know if you remember me. I'm Nick Colter. I was stationed with Jim in Afghanistan. He always told me I should come visit his family, and when Jim's parents, Bob and Ellen, asked me to come…well…I said I would."

As he spoke, sorrow blanketed her features and she took a faltering step away. Her small action sent a myriad of emotions coursing through him.

Grief, anger, sadness, but lying beneath all that, a deep well of guilt at being the one standing here instead of her beloved husband, Jim. He, who had little to live for, had survived and Jim, who had so much to live for, had not.

This is wrong, he wanted to tell her. *And I know it is. I shouldn't be here.*

He shook his head and shifted his weight, wincing as the movement resurrected pain from an injury that had given him a one-way ticket back home.

Behind the pain came the thought that he needed to be back with his unit, doing the job he'd trained for and had done since he was eighteen.

But he had a medical discharge he couldn't work around, and a promise to keep.

Beth wrapped one arm around herself as if trying to hold in her sorrow, her eyes flitting away from him. "I remember you now." She spoke quietly, grief softening her voice. "I saw you at the funeral."

Nick wanted to say something to ease her pain, but any words he might have were too small for the moment. So he stood in front of her, hat in hand, letting his silence say what his mouth couldn't.

Sometimes words couldn't say it all.

"What...what are you doing here?" she asked, still looking away from him.

He was here because as Jim lay dying in his arms, he pleaded with Nick to keep an eye on his wife, to watch over her and make sure she was okay. While Jim's life seeped out of him into the desert sand, his eyes held Nick's with an intensity that branded itself into Nick's very soul as he pleaded with Nick to take care of his family.

But when Nick looked into Beth's eyes, he wondered if this was the time to say all that.

"Mr. and Mrs. Carruthers asked me to come for a visit." He decided to go with the safest reason for now. The visit was true. Bob and Ellen Carruthers had extended the invitation at Jim's funeral when they had found out about Nick's medical discharge from the army.

"That's very considerate of you," she said.

He slipped his hat back on his head, unable to

keep his eyes off her, remembering too well Jim's pictures of her.

In those pictures Beth's blond, curly hair flowed free, her wide violet eyes looked as if they held some secret and her mouth barely hinted at a smile.

Though her features now held the same ethereal quality, they also held sorrow.

"Jim talked about you a lot," he added, struggling with his own grief. "He really loved you."

She took a step away from him, shaking her head and lifting her hand as if pushing him away. "I can't talk about Jim."

"Of course. I'm sorry. I'm sure this is a difficult time for you."

She turned her head aside, hiding her sorrow. "Enjoy your visit with my in-laws," she said. She moved past him and walked to a small car, got in and started it up.

Nick watched her sitting stock-still in the car, her hands gripping the steering wheel as she stared straight ahead, plumes of exhaust swirling around the car.

He wasn't surprised at her reaction. She was still grieving. *He* was still grieving. It had been only eight weeks since his friend breathed his beloved wife's name with his last breath.

Nick clenched his hands and tamped down the sorrow. He wouldn't be any good to Beth or to Jim's parents if he couldn't control his own grief.

For a moment he cursed Jim again. Had Nick done what he always did—went his own way, did his own thing, kept himself from making friends as he usually did—he wouldn't have had to deal with this sorrow.

But when Jim burst into their army tent with his big grin and boisterous personality, he also burst through the walls Nick had carefully built around his heart.

Now Jim was gone and Nick was alone again.

Nick slung his duffel over his shoulder, then limped over the packed trail toward the log house.

Toward Jim's parents and their sorrow.

"And then Jim said to me, I get enough exercise just changing my mind." Nick leaned back in his chair, his arms folded over his chest, his lips curved in a melancholy smile at the memory. "I tried not to laugh, but I still made him do his twenty push-ups."

Dinner ended over twenty minutes ago, but neither Bob nor Ellen Carruthers were in any rush to leave the table. Beth saw them eagerly taking in every story that Nick, Jim's army buddy, had to tell them, drinking in any mention of their beloved son. Throughout dinner their entire attention had been riveted on Nick.

Not that she blamed them. Nick's bearing, his dark hair, piercing blue eyes and strong features created a presence, an air of command that made a person take notice.

She could see why Jim had attached himself to this man. Nick had about him an air of danger, something Jim had always been drawn to. He also seemed to have a quiet strength.

Something she could be drawn to.

She shook the thought off and turned her attention back to the pie she'd been pushing around her plate for the past ten minutes.

"Oh, that sounds just like him." Bob slapped his hand on the table, rattling the plates and forks. "Can't you just hear him saying that, Beth?"

Beth gave her father-in-law a careful smile, avoiding Nick's direct gaze. "I certainly can."

"Jim sure loved his practical jokes," Ellen said quietly. "I'm not surprised that even in that place he found a way to laugh."

Beth's heart softened as she saw the sorrow course across Ellen's features. Once again guilt reared its ugly head, mocking her. She wished she could grieve Jim's death as deeply as her in-laws did. But she couldn't.

The Jim she knew was not the Jim her in-laws often talked about and grieved for. Nor was it the Jim that Nick spoke so glowingly of.

The Jim she knew had come home a couple of times smelling of some other woman's perfume. After pressing him, he had spilled out words of remorse over his infidelity. It was a mistake, he had said. It would never happen again.

And she had believed him. Twice.

The Jim she knew had come back to his parents' ranch full of promises that being around his parents would remind him of who he was supposed to be.

They even went to church the few times Jim was on leave.

Because of the vows she had made, she let herself believe his promises of a fresh start. She wanted her marriage to work. Her pregnancy was a result of her naïveté.

But she also found out that "never again" had meant "only a few weeks." Jim's words, like her father's, meant nothing.

"He often talked about his family." Nick's deep voice broke into her bitter memories and his gaze landed on her. "He especially talked about you,

Beth, and the baby. He looked forward to coming home and seeing you again."

Beth realized this was said for her benefit, and coming on the heels of her own thoughts, the comment was like a knife to her heart.

"He missed you a lot, Beth."

Beth shot Nick a puzzled glance. Once again a slender wisp of hope wafted through her mind. The same hope that had accepted Jim's apologies after his infidelities. The same hope that had taken him back both times.

The refrain of an old song spun through her mind. "Fool me once, shame on you. Fool me twice, shame on me." Except there was no line for "fool me thrice."

She had been such a silly fool.

Nick looked at her with expectancy, but she could only muster a tight smile and Nick, thankfully, turned his attention back to Ellen and Bob.

"He loved you all so much," Nick continued. "I'm really thankful I had a chance to meet you."

"And I'm thankful you took the time to come down here and stay with us," Bob replied. "It means a lot to hear stories about Jim. It's all we've got left." Bob's voice broke a little, and Beth felt a surge of sorrow for her father-in-law.

It didn't matter that Jim had never been the husband to her they thought. He was their only son.

"Oh, my goodness, where's my manners? Nick, would you like some more pie? Or coffee?" Ellen hastily brushed away her tears and got up from the table.

Nick held up his hands as if surrendering. "I couldn't eat another bite. Jim told me your pie was the best I would ever eat, and now I know he wasn't lying."

Beth choked down another bite of that same pie, then took a drink of tepid tea to help get it down. She'd struggled all through the meal to eat enough to keep her in-laws from commenting on her appetite. But each mouthful had been an ordeal.

Her emotions toward her husband were a tangle of pain, anger and confusion, which she struggled to deal with in front of her in-laws. Each time she was with them it grew more exhausting to find a balance between her sorrow over Jim's death and her relief.

Jim's parents didn't need to see the relief.

Though Beth lived only a few hundred feet away from her in-laws, she tried to maintain a boundary and often kept to herself.

But today they'd insisted she come to see Nick's friend. So she'd reluctantly accepted the invitation, then sat through dinner listening to Nick's stories and keeping her feelings in check.

She finished her pie, picked up her plate and stacked Bob's plate on top.

But Nick reached across the table and put his hand on hers.

"I'll help with the dishes."

She could feel calluses on his warm palm. The hands of a soldier.

She jerked her hand back, the plates she held clattering onto the table.

He frowned, obviously puzzled at her reaction. "I'm sorry. I hate to see a pregnant woman working."

"You don't need to look," she said with a touch of asperity she immediately regretted.

She blamed her shortness on the headache she'd been fighting ever since she came back from Shellie's craft store after her doctor's appointment. She'd been working up enough courage all week to talk to her boss about carrying her handmade cards in the store, but when she got to work, Shellie had already left to go to a craft show. So she'd chatted with Isla, the other part-time employee, tidied up the paper racks, reorganized the stamps and set up a new display in the window.

Then, when her few hours of work were over,

she'd made the trip back to the ranch, her brief-case still brimming with homemade cards and her nervousness translating into a headache.

"Now I'm sorry," Beth replied, giving him a quick smile. "I'm just tired."

His crooked grin seemed at odds with his rough and rugged demeanor, but obviously she was for-given. "I think you're allowed to be," he said with a touch of consideration.

Beth held his gaze a moment, surprised at his tone. Not what she'd expect from a friend of Jim.

"You both just sit down. We'll do the dishes later," Ellen said. "Beth, why don't you tell us what the doctor told you this afternoon? We don't get to see much of you, so it's nice to catch up."

"Everything is progressing the way it should," Beth reported, repressing another surge of guilt at her mother-in-law's muted reprimand. "But he wants to see me in a couple of days again, though I don't know why."

"I'm sure he just wants to keep his eye on you, given what you've had to deal with." Ellen gave her a gentle smile.

"But you're feeling okay?" Bob asked, a touch of concern in his voice.

"I saw your light on at twelve o'clock last night,"

Ellen said. "Were you having a hard time sleeping, my dear?"

"I usually do," was all Beth said.

They didn't need to know she stayed up until two o'clock taking apart the cards she had already made, rethinking designs and colors all to impress an absent boss. Like Jim, Bob and Ellen didn't understand how she could spend so much time on her "little hobby," as Jim had called it, so she didn't talk about it in front of them.

Bob leaned back in his chair, his arms crossed over his worn plaid shirt. "So things are okay for you, Beth?"

"Just fine." An awkward silence followed her brief comment and Beth looked down at her clenched hands resting on her stomach. She felt Nick watching her and wished she could leave.

During the entire meal he'd been giving her sympathetic smiles. Poor dead Jim's pregnant widow.

A surefire combination for pity. But she didn't want his or anyone else's pity. She just wanted to get on with her life. And having Jim's friend around wasn't helping. Especially a friend who constantly talked about Jim as if he was a devoted husband and excited father-to-be.

Beth shot a nervous glance at the clock. Her

brother had told her that she had to call him at seven-thirty on the dot if she wanted to connect with him. It was seven-fifteen. Time to go.

She pushed her chair back and ponderously got to her feet. "I'm sorry, but you'll have to excuse me," she said, shooting a quick glance around the table. "I have to make an important phone call."

Ellen frowned her curiosity, but Beth wasn't about to tell her that her conversation with her brother was about her moving off the ranch and into his apartment in Vancouver.

She knew the Carrutherses expected her to stay on the ranch indefinitely, but she couldn't. Especially now that Jim was gone. She had to get on with her life and away from the memories.

"I'll walk you to the house," Bob said, making a move to get up.

"No. There's no need." Beth raised her hand to stop him. "You keep visiting with Nick. I'll be fine."

"I'll walk her to the house," Nick said, standing up and pushing his chair under the table.

She should have quit while she was ahead, Beth thought. She did not want to spend any more time with Nick than she had to. She was tired of smiling at his stories about Jim, tired of how impressed Nick was with Jim's supposed devotion to her.

"I'm okay. Really," Beth protested again.

"I'm sure you are, but it's dark and slippery," Nick said, coming around the table. "And I promised Jim I'd look out for you."

Beth stifled another protest. Going along with his chivalry was the best way to get through this. He would be gone tonight. Soon she'd be living in Vancouver and Nick and Jim and the Carruthers family would be part of her past.

"Thanks so much for dinner," she said to Ellen. "It was delicious."

"You can come anytime, you know," Ellen said, a hopeful note in her voice.

"I don't want to impose."

And before they could tell her yet again that her presence would never be an imposition, she walked out of the kitchen. Waddled, more like.

All the way to the entrance she was far too aware of Nick looming behind her. She quickened her pace, but in spite of his limp he moved surprisingly quick. He had moved past her, pulling her coat off the rack in the entryway. A protest sprang to her lips, but it was probably better, for now, to simply put up with all his hovering.

As he lifted her coat up over her shoulders, his fingers brushed her neck. A tiny shiver danced down her spine and Beth jerked away.

"I'm sorry," he said, his voice gruff. "Just trying to help."

"It's okay." She murmured her automatic reply, wondering why she felt so jumpy around him. Probably because she fell short of his expectations of the grieving widow.

Not much she could do about that. She had shed more tears before Jim died than after.

A brisk wind howled around the yard as they stepped out from the shelter of the trees. Beth pulled her coat closer around her, shivering.

"Are you warm enough?" Nick asked as he walked alongside her, his footsteps crunching on the dry snow.

She wasn't, because her coat was too small and could barely close around her stomach. She didn't want to spend money on another one when she would be moving to a warmer city soon. So she just shivered through the cold.

"I'm plenty warm enough."

They walked in silence toward her house. In the distance a coyote sent a howl up to the sliver of moon hanging just above the mountains. Stars were scattered bits of light in the inky-black sky above them. She felt her tension ease away in the presence of all this peace and beauty.

As much as this place held bad memories, she

knew she would miss it. The peaceful quiet was a welcome antidote to the emotions warring in her soul.

"So how are you managing?" Nick asked as he limped alongside her, his hands in his pockets. "With Jim gone?"

"I'm okay."

"And financially?"

"I've got my…widow's pension and I work part-time in a craft store in town. I used to work as a waitress until my boss told me I had to quit." She worked both places for minimum wage, but every penny was deposited into her escape fund.

Only, now she didn't have to escape anymore. Jim had left her before she could leave him.

"I know I said it before," Nick continued. "But I'm really sorry for your loss. I'm sure it's…hard. What with the baby and all," he said, his voice a rough sound in the quiet evening. "I know Jim looked forward to seeing you again and the baby, of course. Being a family again."

Beth suppressed a burst of anger. Being a family hadn't been high on Jim's list of priorities before he left.

"I'm sure he was," was her noncommittal reply.

They came to the darkened house and Beth shivered again, her steps slowing. She'd forgotten to turn on a light before she'd left for the Carutherses' house. She hated coming home to a dark place.

It meant no one was home and she would be all alone again.

She climbed the single stair to the front door and turned to Nick. In spite of gaining half a foot, she still had to look up at him.

He was good-looking enough and Beth wondered again why he was single. She knew from the few letters Jim had sent home that his friend was thirty-four and had never been married.

Why was she thinking about him? His life was none of her concern. He would be gone by tomorrow and in a week, if all went well, so would she.

"Thanks for walking me back to the house," she said. "I think I can manage from here."

Nick shifted his weight to his other foot and hunched his shoulders as he released a heavy sigh. "Beth...I feel wrong being here...just me. Jim always said he wanted to bring me to see his parents' place, bring me to meet you..." His voice faltered. Then he coughed and composed himself. "I'm so sorry. I wish I could make things better. When...when Jim was dying, he asked me to tell you that he loved you. That he was sorry."

Beth blinked back a sudden and unexpected flush of tears. Jim had said he was sorry so many times that the words had lost their meaning and their power to change her view of him.

"I appreciate you telling me this," she murmured, sensing Nick's need to know he had completed his mission. "Thank you."

Nick cleared his throat again. "I wish I was good with words, but I'm not. I just can't find the right ones to tell you how sorry I am."

Beth looked at him, then released a heavy sigh. "Words are cheap and easy to throw out, so don't worry about not having the right ones."

Nick gave a jerk of his head that Beth supposed was a nod. "Before Jim died he asked me to make a promise to take care of you. And to take care of your baby. I'm not sure how I'm going to keep those promises—"

"Don't say anything more." Beth held up her hand. "I can manage on my own. So I absolve you of whatever promise Jim made you make. You can leave tonight knowing you've done your job. For the rest, I just want to start the next phase of my life on my own."

When she saw the frown on his face she regretted the harsh note that had entered her voice. She'd been so careful to keep things under control. She couldn't let herself be drawn into the uncertain area of words and emotions where she knew she would lose her footing and her way.

"I'm sorry," she said quietly, pulling back from her anger. "Thanks for bringing me to the house. I appreciate you coming and telling me what you told me. As for what Jim told you…well…Jim tended to be kind of dramatic, so don't take what he said too seriously." She stopped, realizing how that sounded. Jim had made Nick agree to the promise while he was dying. Of course it would be dramatic. She sighed and tried again. "I guess I'm saying that it's okay. I understand what Jim was trying to do, but it isn't necessary. So thanks for delivering the message. And…well…goodbye." Since there was nothing more to say, she slipped into her house and shut the door.

She leaned her tired head against the rough wood as Nick's words resonated in her mind. *Jim asked me to watch out for you.*

She closed her eyes, then slammed her fists against the door, trying to find an outlet for the myriad of emotions tangling and twisting through her mind.

"Why did you tell him that, Jim?" she whispered into the dark, wishing her husband could hear her. "You never cared before."

She waited a moment, trying to find equilibrium and trying not to let even the tiniest flicker of hope lull her into believing anything Jim told Nick.

Jim's words meant nothing. They hadn't before he died. They certainly didn't now.

No matter what Nick thought.

Chapter Two

Nick spun away from Beth's closed door, his hands clenched into fists at his sides as he limped down the sidewalk. Why had he offered to escort her back to the house? Why did he put himself through this?

Because after looking at her across the dinner table, after seeing the grief on her face, he couldn't let her leave on her own.

Though she hadn't said anything, in those few moments walking alongside her, looking into her upraised face lit by the moon's soft glow, something elemental had shifted inside him.

Something dangerous and wrong.

He was growing attracted to Jim's widow.

He neared the main house, the heaviness of his guilt and grief weighing him down as much as his injury.

"That was quick." Ellen paused in her task of loading the dishwasher and looked up as Nick stepped into the kitchen. "Is Beth okay?"

"Yeah. She seems to be. I think she just wanted to be alone."

"She spends too much time alone," Bob said, getting up from the table. "We've tried to have her over time and time again, but she gives us one of her reserved smiles and says she'll think about it. Still can't see how she and Jim ended up together." Bob shook his head in puzzlement. "Jim loved to chat and talk and be around people. Beth never says much. Never did."

"Beth is just a quiet girl," Ellen said. "And yes, it would be nice if she opened up to us, but Jim said the same thing. She's just more reserved, that's all. Keeps to herself."

"I'll say," Bob harrumphed, tugging his jeans up over his ample girth. "All she does now is sit at home alone, making those silly cards of hers."

"Cards?" Nick shot Ellen a puzzled look.

"Beth likes to craft greeting cards." Ellen walked to the refrigerator and pulled a card loose from a magnet holding it in place. "This was one she made for my birthday."

Nick took the card, glancing down at the flowers and ribbon and cutout pieces of paper decorating the front. *Happy Birthday* was printed in shiny letters and pasted on a circle on the top of the card.

"Pretty," was all he could say. He flipped it open and glanced over the printed poem on the inside with Beth's signature written on the bottom, then handed the card back. "Looks like she put a lot of work into it."

"Waste of time and paper is what I say," Bob replied.

"It probably keeps her mind off Jim. Though now the poor girl has other things to think about." Ellen pressed her lips together as she traced the raised words on the card.

Nick thought of his own mother and for a moment felt an echo of an older grief. Life was so messed up. He had no parents and Bob and Ellen had no son and here they were together.

Bob cleared his throat. "Let's go sit in the living room." He nodded toward Nick. "We always have devotions there after supper. Do you have time to join us?"

Nick held his gaze as a trace of his former life drifted into his thoughts. His parents always had devotions after supper, as well. They would read the Bible and pray sincere prayers, believing God heard them.

"You don't have to join us if you don't want

to. Beth never has," Ellen said quietly, misunderstanding his silence as she tacked her card back on the refrigerator. "If you have plans for tonight, I understand."

He faltered, wishing he could simply say no. But he was their guest and even though he and God hadn't spent much time together lately, he didn't have to deny their faith. Joining them was the least he could do for his buddy's parents.

Besides, he didn't have anything else to do. Go back to Cochrane to a hotel and from there...

He put the thought aside as Ellen tucked her arm through his.

"You know, I feel as if we know you beyond the few letters Jim would send," she said as they walked to the living room. "When Jim told us your parents had died when you were just a teenager, we started praying for you, too."

"Thank you," he said. The thought that they remembered him in their prayers warmed some forgotten part of his soul. Sure, he didn't believe in prayers anymore, and the fact that Nick was here, and not the son they had also prayed for, proved that.

But yet...

As Nick entered the living room his steps slowed. While the kitchen was cozy and comfortable, this room looked like part of a movie set. The log walls soared up a story and a half. Windows covered one entire wall. Though they were just dark rectangles and triangles now, Nick suspected, given the orientation of the house, that in the daytime one had an unsurpassed view of the mountains.

The room created a sense of space and, at the same time, peace and warmth. For the smallest moment he regretted not deciding to stay here longer.

As Nick looked around he noticed a group of pictures.

"Are those pictures of Jim?" he asked Ellen. "Can I have a look?"

"Of course. Our home is your home." She made the offer as easily as offering him another piece of pie.

His eyes flicked over the pictures. Jim flashing a gap-toothed grin. Jim holding up a fish. Jim wearing a football uniform in high school. Jim in a tuxedo, his arms slung over the shoulders of two attractive women, one of them with dark brown hair, the other a redhead, but neither of them blonde Beth. Looked like high-school graduation.

Beside the gallery a shelf held a formal photograph of Jim in uniform looking more solemn than

Nick ever remembered him to be. And beside that, a wedding picture of Beth and Jim.

He leaned forward to get a better look.

Nick recognized the grin on Jim's face. The same one he often saw when Jim would beat Nick in a video game. The same one he saw on Jim's face just before—

Nick pushed the memory aside, turning his attention to Beth in the photo.

The veil, the white dress and her long, curly hair all combined to give her an otherworldly air. Though she looked stunningly pretty in this picture, the Beth he had just met had a mature beauty that this picture gave only hints of.

He thought of the picture of her that Jim always carried around. She looked as serious in that picture as she did in this one—as serious as she had this evening. He wondered if he would ever see her smile.

"That's the trouble with having only one child—one does tend to take a lot of pictures," Ellen said, coming to stand beside him.

"I'm sure you're glad you did now," Nick said.

Ellen adjusted Jim and Beth's wedding picture. "I just wish we had a few more of Beth, but Jim isn't…wasn't one to take many photographs." She sighed, then brightened. "But now we have a grandchild coming, so I have another reason to take pictures."

"You must be thrilled about that," Nick said.

"I've been knitting and sewing all winter," Ellen said with a note of pride. "Beth doesn't know it, though. I want the gifts to be a surprise."

Beth was lucky to have so much help.

So she doesn't really need yours.

The insidious voice twisted through his mind and he sighed. He had promised.

And what can you possibly do for her? What can you offer her that this family can't? She doesn't even want you around.

Nick gave his head a light shake. He knew that promising Jim he would look out for Beth seemed a vague idea at best. He had come to Alberta with no clear plan other than to see her and to make sure she was okay.

But the trouble was now that he'd spent an evening with her, other emotions worked themselves through his soul.

Attraction and appeal and a desire to protect that had little to do with Jim's promise and more to do with the fact that he'd been intrigued by Beth from the first moment he saw her picture.

Don't kid yourself. You can't take care of anybody. She's not for you.

Nick clenched his hands as his thoughts hammered at his composure.

He turned away from the pictures.

Ellen curled up in a chair on one side of the woodstove while Bob threw another log on the crackling fire. With a heavy sigh, Bob settled into a worn leather recliner opposite Ellen, pulled a book off an end table beside his chair and leaned back.

Nick took this as a hint that they were ready. So he dropped onto the leather couch facing them, leaning forward, his hands clasped together. He felt the way he did whenever he had to talk to his commanding officer. Unsure of the reception, but unwilling to let his uncertainty show.

Bob opened the book, the crackling of the pages the only sound in the easy quiet filling the room.

"I thought I would read Psalm 46," Bob said, pulling out a pair of reading glasses from his pocket and perching them on his nose. "Jim had to memorize this Psalm for one of his Sunday school classes." He took a wavering breath. "I thought it was appropriate, considering the circumstances." He cleared his throat and began. "'God is our refuge and strength. An ever-present help in times of trouble. Therefore we will not fear though the earth give way and the mountains fall into the heart of the sea…'"

As he read, his voice rose and fell. The words and images they brought to mind seemed to ease the tension that had gripped Nick since he stepped out of the cab.

He hadn't wanted to come here and when Beth had told him that she absolved him of his responsibility to Jim, he felt a sense of relief.

Yet he couldn't shake the feeling that he wasn't finished here.

"'…He makes wars cease to the ends of the earth; He breaks the bow and shatters the spear, He burns the shields with fire. Be still and know that I am God…'"

Nick felt the words settle into his soul and, in spite of the cynicism and bitterness that had been his constant companion, here with Bob and Ellen in their home, he felt God's presence and comfort.

"'…the God of Jacob is our fortress.'" Bob paused at the end, the words a gentle echo in the silence that wrapped around them.

Bob kept his gaze on the Bible, his hand resting on the page, as if drawing strength from it. "Ellen and I prayed every day for Jim and for his safety." He sighed and shook his head. "We hoped Jim would come home and eventually come to stay here in the mountains of Alberta, and not die in the mountains across the ocean." He paused, gathering himself. "But God's ways are the best ways and we're not sure what He has in store for us." Bob gave Nick a direct look. "But we are thankful that you could be here, Nick. That you could come to stay with us." Bob sighed, waited another moment then quietly spoke. "Let's pray."

He and Ellen lowered their heads and folded their hands and Nick followed suit.

"Dear Lord, we thank You that we know You are our refuge and strength in this world even though all we see sometimes is sorrow and pain. We thank You that You care for us. Help us as we struggle with Jim's death. Give us strength and help us to understand…" As Bob's voice faltered, a shard of iron entered Nick's soul.

God hadn't heard their prayers for their son's safety, had He? And what about my parents? Where was He when they died?

Yet as Bob prayed Nick found he couldn't hold on to his anger, and in the face of this man's sincere faith and trust in God, his soul softened.

"…but we know that all things work together for good, and we trust that's going to happen now. Thank You for Your word to us that You will never leave us or forsake us. Help us to cling to that word. Amen."

Nick kept his head lowered a moment, Bob's words like a touch of hope in Nick's lonely life.

Jim had said his parents were churchgoers. Nick had assumed their attendance was a community thing the way Jim had spoken of it. The kind of thing rural people did as a way of connecting with each other. Yet when Bob prayed, it was as if he truly believed God listened to what he said. As if Bob and God had a special relationship.

"Jim talked about you a lot, Nick," Ellen said. "And we feel like we know you the way he did. Jim told us that you, like him, were an only child. He said that your parents died when you were eighteen and that you don't have much extended family." Ellen paused, glanced at Bob, then looked back at Nick. "I'm guessing you don't have many obligations yet because of your medical discharge. And I'm sure that you can find work, but I'm also sure you could use the rest. The quiet. So…what I'd like to let you know…what *we'd* like to let you know… is we would love to have you stay for a while. As long as you like or need to. With us."

Nick sat back, surprised. Though Jim had told him his parents were hospitable and generous, he hadn't expected this.

"I…I don't know what to say," was all he could stammer out. He wasn't sure he wanted to make that kind of commitment. When he had received his discharge, he had initially felt as if the ground had been cut out from under him. All he had known since he was eighteen was the army.

Then, once he got used to the idea, a sense of freedom overtook him. He had possibilities and a chance to start over. A chance to put what happened in Afghanistan behind him.

Staying with Bob and Ellen would be a constant reminder of the accident.

And seeing Beth regularly?

Bob leaned forward, his eyes holding Nick's. "We're lonely, too. And losing Jim…" His voice faltered again.

Nick hesitated, digging through his confusion for the right words. "I'm really thankful for the offer…but I don't think I can—"

Ellen held up her hand, a smile tinged with sorrow lifting her mouth. "We don't want you to feel any obligation and we certainly don't want to put any pressure on you, so please don't feel like you have to say yes. We thought it would be good for all of us to spend time together."

His mind skipped back to the ranch he grew up

on. The security of his home life and the love of his parents.

Then he thought of facing Beth every day for the next few days and he shook his head. "I appreciate your very generous offer, but I'm sorry."

Ellen's smile faltered but she nodded. "Of course. You have things to do. I understand. And I'm sure Beth will, too."

Nick thought back to his brief conversation with Beth. How she had "absolved" him of his obligation. He had a feeling that, in her opinion, there was nothing to understand or care about.

"Would you be willing to at least stay the night?" Bob asked, leaning forward, hope in his voice.

Nick bit his lip, then a sigh eased out of him. "Sure. I'll stay the night," he said.

How hard could it be to spare these people one evening of his time?

"Are you sure you only need two weeks here?" Beth's brother asked as Beth shifted the phone to her other ear, plumping a pillow and adjusting a plant while she listened.

Though Art had told her clearly that she had to call at 7:30 p.m. on the dot, when she'd dutifully made the call he wasn't home. Nor was he home at eight or nine.

So she'd called him first thing this morning

and as a result, had woken him up. Not the wisest move, but Beth forced herself to put up with Art's early-morning surliness because he had something she wanted.

A room and a bed in a town house in Vancouver.

"I'm not due for another five weeks," Beth said, forcing herself to speak quietly as she walked around her house, tidying an already achingly neat living room. "I only need two to three weeks to find my own place so I can settle in before the baby is born."

"You sure you don't want to move in with Curt and Denise?"

"Be realistic, Art. You saw how cramped things were when we got together there for Christmas."

"Yeah. I guess you're right."

"And with Mom living there, there's really no room."

Their brother, Curt, and his wife, Denise, lived in a tiny mobile home in a town so small that if a person glanced sideways, they'd miss it. There were no opportunities for Beth there and, as she had told Art, no room in the trailer.

"Okay. You can come. As long as it's only a couple of weeks and it's just you, and no kid. I've got another guy coming after you and I can't have you around if you have a kid."

Beth clutched the phone, pressing back the words threatening to spill out. That the "kid" she carried was his niece or nephew seemed lost on Art. But then, Art had never been the most tactful nor the most considerate of her brothers.

Then a tightening seized her abdomen, as if her baby also protested the situation. She laid a hand over her stomach, as if to settle the child.

"Don't worry, Art. I won't cramp your lifestyle." The angry words spilled out before she could stop them.

"Hey, little sis, I didn't mean it that way," Art said, instantly remorseful. "It's just, well, I'm kind of under the gun at work and things are piling up personally. Well, you know how things are with me and Abby..."

Beth made some appropriate noises even though she had a hard time feeling sorry for a man who had been putting off his wedding date for the past five years.

"So, well, that's the deal. Uh, are you doing okay?" Art asked, giving his version of sympathy. "You know, with Jim gone and all?"

"I'm doing okay," she said, her anger sifting away in the light of his confused concern.

"You still working?"

"Yeah. Part-time at the craft store and I—"

"Becker. Get out of there." Art's sudden yell made her jump. "Hey, Beth. Sorry. Gotta run. Becker's digging in his dog food again."

A click in her ear told Beth that the conversation and Art's sympathy had come to an abrupt halt.

Though she should know better, Beth felt the prick of tears. Neither Art nor Curt were the storybook brothers her friends in school had thought they were. Thirteen years separated her and Art, the youngest of her two brothers. By the time Beth had come into the family, the boys were in their teens, interested in cars, women and anything but a little sister who cried a lot and, as she grew older, loved to dress up and play with dolls. Anything she had to say to them was greeted with grunts, blank stares and commands to get out of their rooms.

And shortly after she turned six, they both moved out, leaving her with a distant father and a mother struggling to keep her marriage together. A failing proposition, as it turned out.

Beth dropped the phone on the table and glanced at the clock. She had to get going if she wanted to meet Shellie at the store this time. She started for the kitchen to prepare her bag lunch just as she heard a scraping sound outside the house.

What was going on?

She opened the door a crack.

A flurry of snow flew through the air, then another, and through it, Beth made out a man, bent over, wielding a snow shovel.

Who…?

Then he straightened and Beth's heart dropped into her boots.

What was Nick Colter still doing here? And why was he shoveling her sidewalk?

"Excuse me. Can I help you?" The question was rhetorical, seeing as how it was he who was supposedly helping her.

Nick brushed some snow off his dark hair and gave her a quick look, his cheeks ruddy with the cold. "I don't think so. Not in your condition."

"So…what are you doing here?"

Nick rested his hands on the top of the shovel and shrugged as he glanced at the piles of snow he had created on either side of her walk. "I'm guessing shoveling snow, but if you want to call it something else…"

"I thought you were leaving last night." The remark came out more bluntly than she had intended, but his unexpected presence unnerved her.

"Me, too." Nick bent over and pushed another pile of snow up, then tossed it easily aside. "Bob and Ellen asked me to stay for a night. They wanted to hear a bit more about Jim, I guess." Nick grunted as he cleared away another space on her sidewalk.

"You don't need to clear my walk." She glared at him, as if to underline her message, but he wasn't looking at her.

"You might not think so," he returned, intent on his work. "But I don't think your baby would appreciate you slipping and falling."

Beth was about to say something more, then changed her mind. She had to get ready for work. Maybe he'd be gone by the time she was done.

But when she stepped out the door the second time, briefcase in one hand, bag lunch in the other, he was cleaning snow off the sidewalk that ran along the front of the house.

He looked up as she closed the door. "The snow here is really packed," he said. "Has it ever been shoveled?"

"I've never shoveled it because it just leads to the back door, which I never use."

Nick stopped his work, his expression puzzled. "You've been shoveling your own sidewalk?"

"Yeah." Why did he sound so surprised? Jim was gone so much she had learned very early how to fend for herself.

"I thought Bob would."

"He's offered, but I take care of myself," she replied, locking the door behind her. She caught him frowning at her again. "Is something wrong?"

"No. Nothing's wrong." He scratched his head. "I just figured you'd be glad for your in-laws' help. I know they're very concerned about you."

"I've just got a lot on my mind."

Nick nodded slowly, glancing at her stomach. "I'm sure you do." Then he looked up at her and she saw a softening in his features that resurrected the shiver she felt last night when his hand brushed her neck. "I wish we could have met under other circumstances. I know Jim always talked about how he wanted to introduce you to me. Show me around the ranch."

She gave him a quick smile, wishing he would stop talking about Jim and her as if they were some storybook couple. "I appreciate that you wanted to follow through on your promise to Jim and that's admirable, but I have to move on."

"I understand, but I also know how much it must hurt to have lost him. I know he loved you so much." His voice held a wistful note.

"Jim was always a good storyteller," she said, skirting the truth with a non sequitur.

"He sure was. When things were really hard and the fighting got close, I used to get him to tell me stories of the ranch and you. How you met, what you were like. He always obliged. And I know it sounds corny, but knowing you were here, waiting for him, made it a bit easier for me." Nick released a short laugh, as if embarrassed of his revelation.

She wouldn't see him anymore, Beth thought. What would it hurt if she gave him just a little bit of what he expected? He just delivered a message from his buddy. It wasn't his fault Jim was not the buddy Nick presumed he was.

"Jim was a great guy," she said. "He took care of me and…I loved him." At one time, anyway, so it was partly true. "I know I'll miss him a lot." More than that she couldn't give Nick. "Thanks again, I guess, for delivering your message." She felt as if she should say a bit more. He had come all this way to deliver a message she didn't want to hear, but he had come. That must have been difficult if, indeed, he and Jim were as close as Nick indicated. "I suppose you'll be gone when I come back?"

"More than likely. Got a few things I need to do. Gotta get on with my life, such as it is."

Beth fidgeted a bit more as a heavy silence rose up between them. A silence holding words that could not be given form. Words that would change too much between people whose only connection was the memory of a man whom they both saw so differently.

She looked into his eyes and saw curiosity behind the vague concern. But she also saw a man who kept a promise by coming here. "I guess this is goodbye," she said, shifting her briefcase under her arm to hold out her hand.

"I hope things go well for you and your baby." He shook her hand, his grip firm, decisive. "Will you let me know what you have when your baby is born?"

"I will."

"I can give you my cell number," he said, pulling out a piece of paper.

Beth paused a moment while he shifted his weight and unzipped his coat. He pulled a pen and a small notepad out of his shirt pocket, scribbled a number on the paper and ripped it out.

She glanced down at the number, then up at him. "Thanks. I'll get Bob or Ellen to call you."

He tipped her a crooked smile. Their eyes held a fraction of a moment longer and to Beth's surprise she felt a remnant of a long-forgotten emotion.

Attraction? Appeal?

She shook the moment away then shoved the

paper in her purse. "Thanks for cleaning my walk."

"You're welcome." He held her gaze for an extra beat, as if he wanted to say something more.

She lifted her hand in a wave, then ambled off. But all the way to her car she felt his gaze on her. It unnerved her and as she got into her car, she felt a spasm in her abdomen.

She pressed her hand against her stomach, arching her back against a surprising jolt of pain. These Braxton Hicks contractions weren't supposed to hurt.

"Easy now," she murmured to her unborn child. "Just bide your time. Everything is going to be okay. He'll be gone by this afternoon."

And with him, hopefully, another reminder of Jim.

Chapter Three

Nick watched Beth's car leave in a plume of exhaust, confusion and frustration vying for the upper spot in his mind.

When she said goodbye, a part of him rebelled. As he looked into her eyes he felt a stirring of a disloyal emotion. He didn't want this to be the end.

But who did he think he was? Not some white knight riding in to save the damsel in distress. He was nothing but trouble and the farther he stayed away from Jim's beloved wife, the better.

He turned back to his shoveling. This, at least, he could do for her.

When he was done, he straightened and a jolt of pain clutched his hip. He clenched his teeth, riding it out. Maybe cleaning her walk wasn't the smartest thing to do.

As he took a long, slow breath, he looked around. His eyes followed the contours of the fields, softened by snow. A cluster of brown dots broke the white expanse beyond the cattle feeders. Some of the more adventurous cows had moved away from the corrals where they were fed and out into the field.

Nostalgia drifted over his mind at the scene. His parents' ranch had been nestled along a lush river valley between two mountain ranges. The fields were long and narrow, rather than open and spread out, but it created the same feeling in his soul.

A yearning for a time when his life had purpose and a center. A time when he had a family.

He tried to laugh away the melancholy feeling as he shouldered the shovel and limped slowly back to the ranch house. It was better this way. When he talked to other men in his unit, men like Jim who had families, they always had the extra worry of wondering what would become of their people if something happened to them.

He had no attachments and no concerns. Today he was heading back to Calgary. Maybe he would rent a motel room there for a couple of nights. Then he'd be off to Vancouver to visit an old friend.

Or not. At any rate, he was leaving today.

"Nick. Nick…"

Nick paused, listening. Was that Ellen's voice he heard over the running of the tractor?

She sounded scared, and he started running.

He hurried past the house, cursing his limp as he rushed toward the corrals and the sound of Ellen's voice.

"Nick, please help."

He clambered over the fence and saw Ellen on her knees, Bob lying on the ground beside the tractor.

"These look really good, Beth. Just beautiful." Shellie laid the cards out on an empty table in the back room of the craft store.

Beth clenched her hands behind her back. "I'm sensing a 'but.'"

Shellie pushed her long red hair back from her face and sighed. "Why are you insisting on keeping yourself so busy?" Shellie glanced down at Beth's stomach. "I mean, you're going to have a baby."

"But I need to keep busy," Beth said.

"Can I give you some advice?" Shellie put her hand on Beth's shoulder. "Jim's been gone less than three months. You're nearly eight months pregnant and you're still coming here and working. You need to let yourself grieve. This silence of yours isn't healthy."

Beth grew cold and taut as Shellie spoke, then turned away. "I don't want to talk about Jim," she said as she sorted through her cards.

"I know how much this must hurt." Shellie continued, ignoring Beth's comment. "And you don't have to try to be so strong all the time. You are allowed to cry. Jim's mom and dad are worried about you. They say you haven't shed a tear since the funeral."

"I'm okay," Beth insisted. "I'm probably still in the denial stage of grief."

"Maybe you are. I still think you need to talk about Jim."

Beth pressed her lips together, holding back the words that at times demanded to be spoken.

Beth had learned the hard way that words didn't change things. Would Shellie believe her if she told the truth about Jim? Would his parents? Dear Bob and Ellen Carruthers whose eyes would drift to her stomach whenever they came to visit, as if to reassure themselves that part of their son lived on in the child that Beth carried.

The child she would take away from them.

Beth knew she could never tell them about Jim. Part of her reluctance was knowing nothing would be gained by taking those memories away from them.

The other was her own shame. She had taken Jim back twice and he had cheated on her a third time. She didn't want anyone to know that.

Thank goodness Nick would be gone by the time she got off work. At least she wouldn't have to face him and hear his stories about how much Jim missed her.

Beth pulled a few more cards out of her briefcase. "I thought if you carried these, people would be interested in finding out how to make them, so I was thinking we could maybe have a Saturday craft class." She slid two cards toward Shellie. "This one," she said, lifting up an intricate card. "I'd love to do a video tutorial on this one. For a potential blog."

As she laid out her plans she could almost feel Shellie's impatience with her reticence washing over her.

"Beth, honey, we have talked about this before. I don't think people would come to the classes. I don't want to do a blog and I highly doubt video tutorials are going to make any difference for us. You're reaching too far."

Ever since Beth started working for Crafty Corners, she had plans and dreams for the store well beyond Shellie's. Her boss had taken the store over from her mother when it was just a hobby store and seemed content to keep the store what it was—a small craft store that sold products for local crafters.

She wasn't sure herself why she bothered trying to persuade Shellie to change the focus of the store when she was leaving. It was just that Beth knew the place had so much potential and it bothered her to see it go to waste.

When Shellie guessed Beth wasn't saying anything more, she turned back to the cards. "I guess I could sell these," Shellie said, picking up some of the Valentine's cards. "And you can stick around for a bit this morning because you're here already, but I want to see you leaving here at noon."

Beth put the rest of her cards back in her briefcase and set it on the ground. "I'll sort out the new inventory," she said, stifling a sigh. She trudged to the back room where the new shipment of supplies had come in, a gentle hope extinguished. She didn't know what she really wanted. For Shellie to be ecstatic about what she had created? For her to be excited?

Because if she had seen any encouragement from her boss, Beth might believe in herself a bit more. Might believe there was a way she could channel her passion for cards and paper crafts into something that could augment her widow's pension. She poured so much of herself into her craft. The cards had started as a way of putting feelings she couldn't express into words, into pictures, into colors and patterns. Her family may not have listened to her, but they did pay attention to her cards.

She gave cards to teachers, to friends, to her family and slowly it became the one constant in her life. The one constant as she followed Jim from one army post to another all over Canada.

Beth had fought the move back to the Carrutherses' ranch, but Jim had been adamant. He wanted her around his family before he shipped out to Afghanistan.

In retrospect, Beth was sure Jim had ulterior motives for the move, but at the time she agreed with it to keep peace.

Mostly she agreed to move because the move didn't affect the plans she had been slowly putting into place.

She was leaving him, moving away and starting out on her own. She had made this decision a week after he shipped out and a week after she found out Jim had cheated on her—again. But she couldn't leave while he was overseas. So she waited until his return so she could tell him to his face.

But Jim didn't come back and she was unexpectedly pregnant and all that lay ahead of her was the uncertainty of motherhood as a widow.

As Beth finished sorting the paper, a feeling of self-pity loomed, like a huge black hole ready to draw her in. A hole she could not edge toward because there was no one to pull her back.

She was alone. She had to be strong for herself and the baby.

Her hands slowed as she stared out the window of the shop, watching the wind toss the snow around the streets of Cochrane. It was winter now, but spring was coming. That was a promise she knew would be kept.

The air felt brisk and cool and the snow crunched under her boots as Beth trudged up the driveway. She was glad she had gone for a walk when she had come home from work. The fresh air cleared the cobwebs of worry and concern from her head.

As she walked closer to the yard she heard the sound of a tractor. She glanced at her watch, then frowned.

Bob usually did the chores in the morning. Not at three in the afternoon. She didn't see his truck when she came home so she had assumed he and Ellen were gone. She shoved her hands in the hoodie she had pulled on over her sweater before she left her house and walked toward the sound, wondering what was going on.

As she approached the corrals where the cows were housed for the winter, she saw the tractor dropping a bale of hay in the feeder along the fence. The tractor turned and faced her, then stopped.

And Nick jumped out of the cab.

She hurried toward him as he vaulted over the fence, running, calling her name.

"What's going on?" she asked. "Why are you feeding the cows?"

Nick slapped his gloves together, a concerned expression on his face. "I had to bring Bob to the hospital this morning—"

"What happened?" Beth stared at him, blood roaring in her ears as she wavered on her feet. Not again, please, Lord, not again.

Nick reached out and caught her by the arm, steadying her. "It's not life-threatening. He was repairing the front-end loader and it came loose and fell on him."

Beth clutched her stomach against a sudden pain. "Are you sure he's okay?"

"He broke his leg, but the doctors set it and Ellen is with him right now."

Beth pressed her hand to her heart, then took a long, slow breath.

Nick frowned, moving closer. "Are you okay? You look a little pale."

"I'm fine. I'm just…it's just…" She couldn't fit her emotions into the uncertainty of words. "You're sure he's okay?"

"Yeah. I tried to call you."

"I left my cell phone at home."

"I came back to do the chores, which didn't get done this morning, so that's why I'm still around."

He sounded a bit defensive, as if unsure of her reaction.

"How long will it take for him to recuperate?" Beth asked.

Nick hunched his shoulders against a sudden gust of wind, then shifted as if to shield her from it. "I don't know. The doctor said he'd be in the hospital for a few days and then lots of physio. He broke his femur, so while not life-threatening like I said, it's still serious."

Beth swayed again, then realized that Nick was still holding her arm. She pulled away. "I should go to see him."

Nick shook his head. "He told me to tell you to stay home. He doesn't want you driving."

"That's silly. I have to go see him." She turned

to go back to the house when Nick caught her by the arm again.

"Give me about half an hour to finish up here and I'll drive you."

She was about to protest when another spasm seized her stomach. What was going on? The doctor had told her everything was fine just yesterday.

"Are you okay?" he asked.

"I think so."

He blew out his breath then his voice grew stern. "Let me drive you to see Bob. I can't let anything happen to you."

Beth drew in a long, slow breath, surprised at the fierce note in his voice. She was about to protest again when she caught his gaze. In that moment she didn't see a man who was being thwarted—she saw a soldier who was used to commanding.

She gave in and nodded. "Okay. I'll go with you."

"I'll come get you when I'm done here."

She nodded again, then walked, slowly back to the house, as if testing every step. But by the time she got there the pain was gone. Before she stepped inside, however, she shot a quick glance behind her.

Nick was watching her, his hands on his hips,

his eyes narrowed. Even from this distance she felt the intensity of his gaze.

She stepped quickly into the house, then made her way upstairs to her craft room. She needed to make a card for Bob. It would keep her mind busy while she waited for Nick.

As she pulled out pieces of paper, the general unease that had held her in its grip slowly eased away. Bob would be okay. He would be fine.

Beth pressed her inked-up stamp onto the card, sprinkled the embossing powder over the words she had just inked, tipped over the card and tapped the leftover embossing powder into the container.

She turned on her heat tool and gently waved it over the powder adhering to the stamped sentiment. Though she had done this countless times, it still gave her the tiniest thrill to watch the loose powder adhering to the image slowly melt and become cohesive—one shiny line of color, in this case deep blue, spelling out the words *Get Well Soon*.

She wasn't sure why she bothered. She knew exactly what Bob would think of the card. He would give her a patronizing smile and set it aside and wonder once again how his son had ended up with someone so quiet, so different from boisterous Jim.

This was the only way she knew to tell him how she felt, however. Spoken words were easily ignored, misunderstood and ignored.

Words written in a handcrafted card had substance and lasted.

Besides, she had to do something to keep her mind off Nick still working on the yard below her. He was supposed to be gone, not running a tractor only a few hundred feet from the house. He made her uncomfortable and he brought expectations she couldn't meet. And with those unmet expectations came guilt she thought she had banished months ago.

She didn't want to pretend to be the grieving widow anymore. She wanted to move on with her life. Leave Jim and the memories of him and the shame he caused her behind her.

The powder melted and she turned off her heat tool and angled the card in the light coming from the window beside her. Not too cute, yet not too elegant. A man's card, if there was such a thing. She resisted her usual urge to tie a ribbon on it, then picked up her pen and a piece of scrap paper.

She hesitated, the pen hovering above the paper. As always, the words took time coming as she struggled to imagine what Bob would want to hear from her.

She glanced sideways out the window overlooking the yard. From here she saw Nick still feeding the cows, though it looked as if he was filling the last feeder. As he got out of the tractor he walked through the crowd of animals, his movements deliberate and slow. She wondered how he'd got his limp. Wondered what kind of action he'd seen.

He cut the twine on the bale, ignoring the cows milling around him. Then he stepped back, winding up the strings he had just pulled off, his eyes on the animals with their heads now buried in the feeder.

Then he turned as if looking at the mountains. His hands stopped, falling to his side as he stood, perfectly still. Then, with a shake of his head, he returned to the tractor.

What had he been thinking in that moment? What was going through his mind?

He seemed to be so comfortable around the animals. So relaxed. She thought of what he had said last night at Bob and Ellen's. How he had grown up on a ranch just like Jim had.

Except he seemed to enjoy the work a lot more than Jim ever did. She couldn't recall Jim ever helping his father or even talking about the ranch with his father. The only reason they moved back to the ranch was for her sake, Jim had said. So she could have a home base and be near his parents.

Nick got back into the tractor, reversed and drove it past the other groups of cows. A few moments later he disappeared behind the shed and Beth knew he was parking the tractor, which meant he'd be here soon.

She turned her attention back to the blank piece of paper in front of her. What words could she put in there that would make Bob understand that she appreciated him? What words would be sufficient to let him know her turmoil at being here with such good people when their own son was so different from them?

She tapped her pencil on the paper, fragments of phrases spinning through her mind.

I appreciate your help…

Thanks for your support…

I wish I could tell you how I really feel…

Hope you get better in time for me to move away…

Beth tried to keep thoughts of her future at bay, but they crowded back into her mind, shoving and pushing and demanding attention.

What could she say to the man whose grandchild she would be taking away?

She pressed her fingers to her eyes, trying to

marshal her thoughts, then pushed aside her practice paper, picked up her pen and wrote directly on the card. She waited for the ink to dry before she slipped the card in the matching envelope she had crafted.

She hoped he would read it and understand what she was trying to say.

A knock on the door downstairs pulled her away from her tangled, tiring thoughts.

"Come on in," she called out, getting up. Her back throbbed more than when she had sat down. She arched her back against the pain, then shuffled to her bedroom across the hall to get ready.

She pulled her hair back again, tightening the elastic that held it in place. She did a quick check in the mirror. Her eyes looked too big, her mascara was smudged and she needed some more lipstick.

She grabbed a tube from her makeup basket, then caught herself. She was just going to the hospital. She dropped the lipstick tube, then spun away from the mirror and got the card.

As she carefully made her way down the stairs, Nick hurried forward and took her by the elbow. She was about to pull away, then realized how foolish that would be.

"Thank you," she murmured, avoiding looking up at him.

"Is this your coat?" he asked, pulling it off the newel post of the staircase.

She nodded and reached for it but he already held it up for her. Again she felt a brush of disquiet when he settled the coat on her shoulders.

"Are you okay?" he asked when she pulled away again.

"Just not used to being treated like this," she said with a jerky laugh, hoping to dispel the curious feelings he created in her.

"Really?" he asked with a puzzled frown. "Jim struck me as such a gentleman. He was always helping out the women at the base."

Beth slipped the card she'd finished into her coat pocket and emitted a humorless laugh. "Of course he was."

Nick's frown deepened and Beth realized how that must have sounded.

Nick reached past her and opened the door. She tried not to look at him as she went through. Tried not to be aware of him as he walked beside her.

He made her uncomfortable because his presence brought up memories of Jim. That's all, she told herself.

But as she gave him another sidelong glance and caught him looking at her, the faint quickening of her heart told her something else.

Chapter Four

Nick tapped his fingers on the steering wheel of the truck he had borrowed from Bob. His eyes were on the road ahead, but part of his attention was on the woman sitting beside him.

He didn't usually have a hard time making conversation with women, but Beth was a puzzle he didn't know how to solve.

Bob and Ellen eagerly listened to any story he had to tell about Jim, tears slipping down their cheeks at times. Beth didn't seem to want to hear anything he had to say about Jim.

Maybe this was her way of grieving but there was something unhealthy about her reaction.

"So, how long have you been on the ranch?" he asked finally, wanting to make some kind of conversation to fill the awkward silence.

"Jim moved me here three weeks before he shipped out to Afghanistan."

"He was based at Suffield, wasn't he?"

Beth nodded, staring straight ahead, her arms folded over her stomach.

"I know he said it made him feel more relaxed, knowing you were at the ranch with his parents. He said he would have worried so much more if you had been somewhere else."

In spite of Beth's lack of response, Nick carried on. It was as if he had to keep Jim present between him and Beth.

Because, if he was honest with himself, his own feelings for Beth were shifting, changing. And not in a way he wanted to acknowledge.

"Whenever we drove together, I'd ask Jim about the ranch," Nick continued. "He loved telling me how he'd go hiking and riding. He was really glad you were here." Nick shot Beth another sidelong glance, but she looked straight ahead, a curious smile playing across her lips. Was she recreating happy memories? Should he continue? "He talked about you, too. How much he missed you. He loved you a lot."

Still no reply from her, but when he shot her another quick glance to check her response he thought he caught the glint of a tear in her eye.

Then she blinked and it disappeared and he wondered if he imagined it.

Nick shifted in his seat. Should he say more or turn on the radio to break the silence?

"So, how do you know about feeding cows?" Beth finally spoke up. "You seem pretty comfortable using the tractor."

Cows? Tractors?

After what he told her about Jim, she wanted to talk about the ranch? With a mental shrug, he figured he'd oblige. At least it was conversation.

"I grew up on a ranch in British Columbia," Nick said. "I used to help my dad all the time, just like Jim. In fact, that connection got us together in the first place."

"Really?"

"Yeah. The first time I met him, he came bursting into the tent and dropped his cot in the empty space beside me and told me that he was a simple farm boy named Jim Bob. I thought he was joking."

"No. That's his real name. He never liked it," Beth said.

"I got that," Nick said, encouraged by even this small admission of hers. His own thoughts drifted back to that first meeting. Nick had, up until then, kept to himself. He always had, but Jim changed that and then Jim died.

He pushed the thought away and tried to continue.

"Once he found out I grew up on a ranch, too, we compared stories. We always had lots to talk about while we were on patrol. Anything to keep a balance between watching out and being paranoid. And anything to keep awake. The trips between the base and Kandahar Airfield are long and tense so Jim would talk about you. Over and over again."

He glanced over at her but again got nothing more than a puzzled frown.

Frustration gnawed at him at her lack of response.

Though, he had to admit, now he knew what Jim felt like when he first got to know Nick. Jim often accused him of being hard to talk to, as well.

"I'm just glad I can help Bob out right now," he said, going back to the topic she'd introduced. "Made me realize how much I missed being on the ranch." Though he hadn't counted on spending the extra time here, working with the cows brought him back to happier times in his life.

Beth frowned. "So why aren't you visiting your parents?"

The question was legitimate, but it touched on

an old pain and Nick waited a moment before answering.

"They died when I was eighteen."

"I'm so sorry. I didn't know."

"It happened a long time ago. You've got a lot more to deal with than I do."

Another awkward silence followed his comment and Nick felt a burst of frustration. Some kind of support he was being. Why did Jim ever think he could do this?

He shot Beth a quick glance, but she looked ahead at the road, her expressionless face in profile against the snow-covered fields that slipped past.

Jim had told Nick over and over how much he loved Beth and how he wished he could be home with her and how once he did, he wouldn't leave.

Yet she seemed so stoic. So unemotional. She had to be full of hurt and pain.

"Beth, I know you're struggling with grief. And I know it's hard." He blew out his breath, wishing he was a praying man. Because right about now he could use some divine guidance on how to talk to a grieving widow. "I don't know much about psychology, but if there's one thing Jim taught me, it's that it's a better thing to open up, to let people know how you're feeling than it is to keep everything to yourself."

He waited for a response, but got nothing.

"I know it will take time—" He was interrupted by a sudden cry from her. He shot her a concerned glance.

She was bent over, breathing hard.

"What's the matter?" Nick slowed, turned on the hazard lights and pulled over to the side of the road. Snow swirled around the truck. "What's happening?"

Beth just held her hand up, as if telling him to keep his distance. "Nothing. I don't think—"

Whatever she had to say was cut off by her gasp of pain.

"Beth, what's wrong?"

She clutched her stomach. "I'm not sure," she answered. "It's okay. It's gone now."

"We've got to get to the hospital," he said, pressing his foot against the accelerator as he got back onto the highway.

"Well, yeah."

"For you."

She shook her head. "It's probably false labor or something like that."

"How do you know?"

"I just know," she said.

She pressed her hand against her stomach as if to test what was happening, then shot him a triumphant glance. "Nothing. Everything is fine."

"You use 'fine' a lot."

"It is what it is. I am fine."

He wasn't so sure, and the rest of the way to the hospital he kept glancing from her to the road, every nerve alert.

It was like driving in Afghanistan all over again, he thought, forcing his hands to unclench the steering wheel, making himself relax his tight jaw.

He didn't need to be tense. This was Alberta. He didn't have to worry about road bombs or snipers. The roads were clear and there was no enemy. He didn't need to live with the same fear he'd lived with there.

Yet by the time they got to the hospital, Nick felt as if he'd driven two hundred miles instead of twenty. His hands felt clammy and a faint line of sweat dampened his hairline.

You're okay, he reminded himself as he parked the truck, then walked around the side to help Beth out. *You got her here.*

She ignored him when he opened the door, but he took her arm anyway. She put one foot on the ground, went to take a step and then buckled.

Nick caught her under the arms, his heart hammering in his chest. "Beth, what's wrong?"

She closed her eyes, leaning against him for a moment, her head resting on his shoulder.

Nick held her as an unexpected surge of protectiveness washed over him in a wave so strong it almost knocked him over, too.

She looked so small, so fragile, and when she looked up at him with pain distorting her features, he wanted to sweep her up in his arms and carry her to safety.

"I'm bringing you to the emergency room," he said.

She only nodded, her eyes wide with fear.

He supported her as they walked, his arms holding her as he cursed the limp preventing him from carrying her inside.

"The baby is not supposed to come yet," she cried. "I'm not ready. It's not supposed to come yet."

"We're at the hospital," he said, making surprisingly quick progress over the slippery sidewalk.

Then she clutched his arm. "Please, don't leave me alone."

Her plea dived into his soul. She couldn't know it, but her husband had uttered the exact same words only a couple of months ago.

Nick's heart hammered in his chest and as he

walked, he said the same thing to her that he had said to Jim.

"I've got you. It's okay. Everything is going to be all right."

They got to the doors of the hospital and suddenly she was doubled over, breathing hard. "I can't walk. I just can't," she cried.

Nick couldn't leave her here to get help. He ignored his limp, swept her up into his arms and carried her into the hospital when the automatic doors slid open.

As he limped into the emergency department, a panicked prayer leaped to his lips.

Please, Lord, please watch over her. Please don't take her away, too.

He was greeted by a pleasant woman who looked at him as if a man carrying a pregnant woman was the most normal thing in the world. The sight of her pleasant, calm face soothed him a bit.

"She's about eight months pregnant. She's having her baby," he called out. Then everything changed.

Within seconds Nick laid Beth on a hospital bed in the emergency room. A doctor swept the curtain across the front of the cubicle aside and a nurse followed him, swishing the curtain back in place.

"Are you the father?" the nurse asked as the doctor began to examine Beth.

He was about to say no when Beth cried out again, her hand flailing out as if trying to reach for something.

Nick caught it and Beth's fingers wrapped themselves around his hand with a strength that belied her small frame.

He shouldn't be here, Nick thought, hanging on to her hand. This wasn't his place. Jim was supposed to be at Beth's side, supporting her, not him.

But Beth wouldn't let go of his hand and he found, to his surprise, that he didn't want her to.

"How far along is she?" the doctor asked as the nurse took her blood pressure.

"A couple of weeks shy of eight months," Nick said, wincing as Beth clung to his hand.

"We have to get her to Labor and Delivery," the doctor said. "We can triage her there." He glanced at Beth's chart. "Page her ob-gyn."

As the doctor gave his orders, Beth's eyes locked on Nick's, her hand squeezing his even tighter. "Please don't leave me. Don't let me be alone."

Nick glanced up at the doctor who shook his head. He looked down at Beth, placing his other hand on top of hers. "I'll be waiting," he said. "I'll be right here."

"No. Please, Nick, I can't do this alone," she called out, grabbing with her other hand. "Please. Please, I can't do this. I just can't. It's too soon. Everything will change." The fear in her voice caught Nick.

He pressed her hand against his chest, standing close to her as she started to hyperventilate.

"Beth. Look at me. Beth."

She opened her eyes, then locked her broken gaze on his.

"You can do this," he said, lowering his voice, holding her panicked gaze. "The baby is just a bit early. You'll be fine. The baby will be fine."

Beth's grip loosened just a bit and her breathing slowed.

"That's a good girl," he murmured.

She looked so forlorn, lying in the bed, her blond hair a curly tangle around her face.

He gave in to an impulse and gently brushed her hair back from her face, his hand lingering to comfort her. Her skin felt soft against his callused hand and he cupped her cheek.

"It's okay. You're in good hands."

As she held his gaze, something elemental and powerful stirred in his chest. He wanted to sweep away all her pain and fear and sorrow. He wanted to drag her into his arms and do exactly what Jim had asked him to—protect her from whatever ordeal she had to face. Be at her side and watch over her.

"I'm sorry, sir, but we have to move her now," one of the nurses was saying, her tone gentle.

"I'll wait for you," he said to Beth, locking his eyes on hers. "I'll be right out the door, waiting."

Then he stepped aside, reluctantly tugging his hand loose from Beth's clinging fingers.

She reached out again, but the nurse was raising the bed's side rails, and with a flurry of activity they all left.

Nick watched the gurney hurrying down the hallway to another part of the hospital, feeling as if something precious had been taken away.

"I can give you directions to where they're going," a nurse said behind him. "If you want to wait for her."

"I'm not her husband." Then, just in case the nurse might think something entirely different, he added, "He's dead. I was with him."

"Then for sure she'll want to know you're waiting." The nurse nodded as if to encourage him. "She sounded like she really wants you there."

Nick blew out a sigh, the panic in Beth's voice reverberating through his mind.

Then he made a sudden decision and went in the direction the nurse had indicated. He may not belong there, but Beth had wanted him and for now, that was enough.

"It's a boy."

Beth heard the news and fell back on the bed. She had a baby boy.

She heard the doctor murmuring something. The nurse's response was muffled.

"Is everything okay?" she called out, a new anxiety building. "Is the baby all right?"

A nurse came alongside her and Beth turned to her, fear roaring through her like a storm she couldn't find her way through.

"Is the baby okay?" she gasped.

"Considering how early he is, he's doing very well. Here, you can hold him for just a bit."

Then a tiny bundle of warm flannel wrapped around her baby was laid on her chest. His tiny face, red and wrinkled, peeked out of the blanket. His eyelids were bruised, his cheeks purple, and as she held him a dozen emotions moved like a kaleidoscope through her head.

He was so small. So precious. How was she

supposed to take care of this child? How was she supposed to manage as a single mother?

Then his hand came loose from the blanket and it reached out. Fingers so small they could hardly be real, spread out like a tiny trembling starfish.

Beth put her pinky into his palm and his fingers caught her finger and her heart in a fierce grip. Beth's heart stilled and behind the quieting of her fears, emotions so huge, so overwhelming, welled up and she wanted to hold this precious, beautiful baby close to her and never, ever let go.

"He's amazing," she whispered, wonder and love washing over her in waves so strong they threatened to engulf her.

"I'm sorry. We have to put him in the isolette now."

Beth clutched him closer to her as the nurse reached out for him. "Not yet," she pleaded. "Please not so soon."

"You'll be able to see him again. But for now, both of you need some rest."

"But he's okay? He's going to be okay?" Beth asked as she reluctantly relinquished her hold on her baby boy.

"He's just fine." Then the nurse smiled. "Have you decided on his name?"

Beth lay back on the bed. "Kyle. His name is Kyle Bob Carruthers."

Her son would be proud to carry his grandfather's name.

And Kyle? Simply a name that she liked.

"Nice name," the nurse said. "He looks like a Kyle."

Another nurse came to the head of the bed. "We'll bring you to your room now," she said.

"But my baby—" Beth tried to sit up.

"We have to keep him in an isolette for just a while. We need to monitor him—"

"He can't be alone." Beth tried to still the panic rising in her voice. "I need to be with him."

"It's okay, Beth. We'll be watching him and bringing you to see him when we can," the nurse said, her voice reassuring. "You need rest and we need more time with him. When you're able to get up, you can come and see him."

The nurses helped Beth onto a gurney and they wheeled her out of the delivery room and away from her baby, each roll of the wheels like a wrench on her heart.

To her surprise she felt the warm trickle of tears sliding down her cheeks as other emotions superimposed themselves over her initial euphoria.

Now what was she going to do? All her well-laid

plans had been swept away in the past few hours. She was supposed to move and start a new life before Kyle was born.

What would she do now?

"Your baby is fine, honey," the nurse pushing the gurney said, giving Beth a smile. "He just needs extra care for the next while. That's all."

Beth just nodded as she watched the ceiling slide past her. She didn't want to tell the kindly woman that her tears were a mixture of the after-effects of having the baby and a sudden onslaught of anxiety.

Could she really take care of Kyle and herself? Could she really strike out on her own and manage? She knew thousands of other single mothers had, but she was sure many of them felt the same.

She closed her eyes, her thoughts seeking comfort from someone or something larger than her. She wanted to pray.

Would it make any difference? God hadn't listened before, why should he now?

Prayers were just words. And words meant nothing.

She was truly on her own.

She drew in a shaky breath as she heard doors sliding open and then the lights from above were no longer shining directly on her. Something blocked the light.

"Beth. Beth."

Her eyes flew open and Nick was beside her, walking alongside the gurney, his eyes intent on her, his head bent over her.

"Hey, I heard you did good," he said.

She stared up at him. "You're still here."

He smiled gently and nodded. "I thought I would wait. Nothing else to do."

She blinked, trying to comprehend. "But you didn't have to—"

He took her cold hand in his, his warm palm rough, strong and surprisingly reassuring. "You asked me to stay."

They had met only yesterday and he had stayed because in a moment of panic and fear she asked him to? Beth closed her eyes, humiliation washing over her as she remembered her outburst, her pleading.

"Sorry about that," she said, turning her head away. "Blame it on the hormones. You didn't have to take that seriously. I'm sorry I wasted your time."

He didn't reply, but to her surprise, he didn't leave, either. He still walked alongside the bed. Still held her hand.

Beth knew she should pull her hand out of his, but his touch was comforting and right about now she could use all the comfort she could get.

"Here's your room," the nurse said, her voice bright and cheery. "You get to be by the window."

The nurse pulled the curtains around the bed and was about to help Beth into the bed, but Nick was right there, easing her over.

The nurse pulled the blanket up and over, and weariness dropped over Beth, pushing her back against the mattress.

"So what did you have?" Nick asked, still hovering at her side.

"A boy," she whispered, staring up at the ceiling, still trying to get her body reconnected with her mind and emotions. "A little boy."

"Really." Nick sighed. "Jim was hoping for a boy."

In spite of her weariness, she felt a twinge of frustration. Would he have? If Jim hadn't gone overseas would he even have been around by now? Would she have stayed?

She glanced over at Nick, catching the look of sorrow on his face.

"He even had a name picked out," Nick was saying, his mouth lifted in a melancholy smile.

Beth had enough. She held up her hand. "Please don't tell me. I can't…I just can't…"

To her surprise, Nick took her hand in his again. "Of course not. I'm sorry."

Beth's initial reaction was to pull her hand back, to retreat into herself as she always did, to tell Nick that he had it wrong. But it felt so good to have him at her side when, in her vision of this birth, she had always been alone.

She would be again, but for now, just for now, she needed to have him here. To have him holding her hand and being an unexpected support.

A movement past the curtains caught her attention and then there was Ellen at her side, her face beaming, her eyes bright with tears.

"Oh, my dear Beth," she said, lightly touching Beth's cheek. "I came as quickly as I could. You poor girl. How are you doing?"

"I'm okay. Tired."

"Of course you are." Ellen glanced over at Nick, then at his hand holding Beth's. "And poor Nick. Two trips to the hospital in one day."

"How's Bob?" Nick asked, releasing Beth's hand.

Beth felt a moment of loss when he did.

"He's doing okay. He's still in a lot of pain, but they're managing it." Ellen turned back to Beth.

"But oh, he'll be so happy to find out about the baby. Is everything okay? What did you have?"

"A little boy," Beth said, weariness clawing at her. "The nurse said he's okay for now."

"What did you decide to name him?" Ellen's eyes, bright with expectation, rested on Beth.

"Kyle. Kyle Bob Carruthers."

Ellen's surprise was so fleeting Beth might have imagined it, but then Ellen smiled.

"Bob will be thrilled." She laid a cool hand on Beth's cheek. "Thank you."

Beth nodded, knowing that Ellen wondered why she hadn't named the baby after Jim. Then the headache that had started with her baby's arrival opened in her head, layered and complex and wearying beyond belief.

She couldn't think. She couldn't speak. To her shame, tears slithered from her eyes again, down the sides of her face.

"We should go," she heard Nick say quietly.

She wanted to thank him for being there, for his consideration, but even that had become too much for her.

Then, sleep descended, blocking everything else out.

The chatter of gunfire, the boom of an explosion. Dust and dirt and heat washed over him in waves.

He looked desperately through the tangled metal of their truck for Jim. Where was he? Nick had to get him home. Get him to his wife. But Nick couldn't open his eyes. Couldn't focus as he struggled to pull open the mangled door. Black Hawks circled overhead, the whup-whup of their blades beating out a steady rhythm. Jim lay inside the truck. He had to get him out.

"Nick. Nick."

A woman's quiet voice wafted over the noise and pain.

"Nick, wake up." He felt a soft hand on his shoulder.

Adrenaline surged through him and he jerked awake, on his feet before he even knew what was going on.

He focused on the woman standing in front of him, her blond hair loose around her heart-shaped face, like a golden halo.

The fog of sleep slowly lifted.

Beth. Jim's wife stood in front of him. Nurses in scrubs strolled past, giving him puzzled looks. He heard the muted beeps of monitors just beyond a set of double doors.

"Nick, you're in a hospital in Calgary," Beth's quiet voice reassured him.

His heart slowed its heavy pounding as he blinked his eyes and brain into focus.

Beth stood in front of him, her hand pressed to her heart, but her expression looked more concerned than alarmed.

"You're okay," Beth said. "We're in the waiting room just outside NICU. Ellen came with me to see Kyle. I woke you up because you were having a nightmare."

Nick shoved his hand through his hair, as the adrenaline slowly wore off and the memories of Afghanistan eased away. "I'm sorry," he mumbled, dragging his hands over his face, struggling to wake up.

"It's okay. Jim used to react the same way when he came back from a tour." Beth eased herself into the chair behind her.

She wore a blue cotton robe over a blue-and-white hospital-issue nightgown. Lines of weariness were etched around her mouth but in her eyes he saw a light he had never seen before.

It gave her a delicate beauty that gave his heart a lift.

"How do you feel?" he asked, unable to look away from her.

"I'm tired, of course, but having Kyle…" Her voice trailed off after she spoke her baby's name, as if she couldn't find the words to explain what she had just experienced. Then she gave him a tentative smile. "Thanks for bringing me here. For... for being there."

"It's okay. Of course I would bring you. And as for staying..." He shrugged, not sure she wanted to talk about that moment when she had called out for him. He didn't quite know what to think of the fierce desire to protect her that had less to do with Jim's request than his own need to be at her side.

"It meant a lot," she said quietly, her eyes connecting and holding his.

He didn't look away. Didn't want to.

Nick felt an urge to touch her. To connect with her. His hand twitched at his side and as he lifted it the doors to the NICU swished open. Reality intruded into the moment in the form of Beth's mother-in-law, Ellen.

She came to Beth's side and put her hand on Beth's shoulder, her eyes moist. "Kyle is so beautiful. I can hardly wait until Bob is strong enough to see him." She swallowed then shot an apologetic glance at Nick. "I'm sorry for being so emotional. It's hard seeing Jim's boy knowing that Jim never will."

Beth simply nodded and Nick guessed this was a difficult moment for both of them.

"You look tired, my dear. You should try to get some rest," Ellen said to Beth.

Beth nodded again but Nick saw her eyes flick to the door of the NICU—as if she would rather be back there, with her son.

The sight warmed his heart.

"I suppose we should get back to the ranch," Ellen said to Nick. "Beth should rest and Bob is down for the night."

"Of course." Nick hesitated, as if waiting for Beth to say something more, but her entire attention was focused on the doors separating her from her son.

Nick grabbed his coat from the chair he'd been sitting in while he'd waited for Ellen to see Kyle. He shoved his arms through the sleeves. "Did the doctor say when you'll be coming home?"

Beth dragged her gaze back to Nick. "I'm being discharged tomorrow."

"And Kyle?"

"He'll have to stay here until his weight comes up or…" Beth's voice faltered and she shot a puzzled glance at Ellen. "What else did the doctor say?"

Ellen gave an apologetic shrug. "I can't remember, honey. Seeing little Kyle in that bed with all those monitors attached to his tiny body felt overwhelming enough." Ellen pressed her hand to her mouth as if even the thought was too much for her. "I'm sorry. I'm not much help to you."

Nick wasn't surprised. Poor Ellen had been given a lot to deal with the past several hours.

"I'll find out tomorrow," Beth told Nick.

"I'll be coming tomorrow anyway. To bring Ellen," Nick assured her.

Was that relief on her face? Or had his imagination put it there?

Ellen hesitantly touched Beth's shoulder, as if she would have preferred to give her daughter-in-law a hug. "What shall I bring you for tomorrow?" she asked instead.

Ellen glanced at Nick and he got the hint that she wanted to be alone with her daughter-in-law a moment.

"I'll be waiting in the lobby," he said to Ellen. Then he glanced at Beth. "Congratulations, Beth."

But as he walked away, he wished he could stay.

He dismissed the thought. He wasn't Beth's husband and he had no right to be at her side.

In spite of his growing feelings toward her.

Chapter Five

Beth slipped on the clothes Ellen had brought, thankful and surprised that they fit. She pulled her hair out of her ponytail and tugged the brush through her curls. She made a face at her image in the mirror of her hospital bathroom.

Pale cheeks. Watery eyes. Dull complexion. Hair a tangle of curls that wouldn't settle.

You just had a baby. What do you expect?

Unbidden came the thought of Nick seeing her like this.

Why does that matter?

Ever since she had come out of the delivery room and found Nick there waiting, she'd been unable to keep him out of her thoughts. She vividly remembered how it felt to see him waiting for her when she came through those doors feeling so alone. How it felt to be carried by him into the emergency ward.

How it felt to have his support. His strength.

When her mother called to tell her she couldn't come until tomorrow, Beth was surprised at how much it hurt.

She had hoped, on one level, that her mother would be eager to be here. Would come when she heard the news. But her brother Curt wasn't able to bring her until later and her other brother, Art, figured he should wait until Kyle was out of the hospital, which, essentially, was code for "too busy to come yet."

But Nick had been here. Nick, who barely knew her, had been the one who brought her to the hospital and was here again today.

He was there for her when she needed him.

"There you are."

The voice of the man she had just been thinking about startled her and she dropped her hairbrush.

He reached for it just as she bent over to get it and for a moment their fingers brushed. Beth drew back as if his touch burned her and she caught his wry look as he handed her the brush.

"You okay?" he asked, a puzzled note in his voice.

"Just feeling a bit tired." She hoped he would take the explanation at face value. She wished she could explain her jumpiness around him on hormones, but something else lurked beneath the surface of her reaction to him.

Attraction?

"I'm not surprised. You've had a tough go." He shifted his weight, his presence dominating the tiny hospital room. "I imagine you'll want to see Kyle again before you go?"

"If you don't mind." Beth bit her lip at the thought of her baby still lying in the isolette in NICU. She had spent the whole day with Kyle, holding him whenever she could, feeding him whenever he was hungry. And it was never enough.

"Of course. I'm sure it's going to be hard enough to leave without him."

"Thanks for understanding." She gave him a trembling smile, then moved past him and down the hallway, stifling the tears that threatened each time she thought of leaving her baby here.

She got to the doors of NICU and was about to go in when she turned to Nick, who stopped by the chairs in the waiting room just outside the NICU. He looked past her to the doors and she gave in to an impulse. "Do you want to see him?"

Nick's startled look made her wish she hadn't

offered. Why would a single guy, an ex-soldier, want to see some poor widow's baby?

"That'd be great," he said with surprising enthusiasm. "Am I allowed?"

"As long as you come with me, you can see him."

"Great. Let's go."

He followed her through the double doors. Once inside, Beth showed him the hand sanitizer and handed him a gown. Then she strode quickly down the hallway as she tied the strings of her own gown, part of her attention on her baby waiting for her, but the other part on the man following her. He loomed over her and she realized how tall he was. How broad his shoulders were. He seemed to overpower the space he took.

"It seems a bit overwhelming at first," Beth said over her shoulder as she turned into another room. "The nurses tell me that Kyle's situation isn't as serious as some of the babies here."

They came to the entrance of NICU and Beth hesitated just a moment. Yesterday she had almost broken down at the thought of her baby in the intensive care unit.

But after spending a day with her child, it wasn't as daunting. Kyle was doing well, his nurse had assured her repeatedly. His presence here was part of the precautions necessary with a premature birth.

As she stepped inside, Beth nodded at Lindsay, another mother, hovering over her own baby's isolette.

"Congratulations," Lindsay said to Nick as they passed her station. "Your son is a very beautiful little boy."

It isn't like that, Beth wanted to protest, but it was too much trouble to correct Lindsay's assumption. One small part of her liked the idea that for even a tiny moment, she wasn't seen as the tragic widow. That she had someone with her.

Beth greeted Kyle's nurse, who was making some notes on Kyle's chart, then turned her attention to her baby boy. This time it was easier to ignore the beeping of the bank of monitors lining the wall. This time it seemed easier to see past the tubes connected to Kyle, to the little body that was her son.

This time she had Nick with her.

The gown the nurses had put on him dwarfed Kyle's tiny body. He lay on his back, his arms splayed out, his tiny fingers curled over his palms, his head turned toward Beth. His mouth was a tiny pucker of pink and as she watched he moved his lips, as if sensing she might feed him.

Beth laid her hands on the plastic covering, her heart softening at the sight of her son, her arms aching to pick him up and hold him. "He may look a little funny," she said to Nick, who now stood across from her, "but I think he's beautiful."

Nick didn't say anything and Beth glanced up, wondering why he was quiet.

He stood with his hands behind his back, a soldier at ease, his yellow gown askew. But his entire attention was focused on Kyle. And to Beth's surprise, she caught the glint of moisture in his eyes.

"It's amazing," he said quietly. "I know he's small, but I can't believe he was once a part of you. Now he's his own person."

What he said made Beth smile. It was as if he took her thoughts and wrapped words around them, making them clearer than she could.

Nick took a step closer, his entire attention riveted on her baby. "It's a miracle. Life is such a miracle. So fragile, yet here he is. I wish Jim could see him. He talked constantly about the both of you."

Regret shivered through Beth. She didn't want Jim's memory intruding on this moment. But she had to acknowledge what Nick was saying.

"I...I wish he could, too." She spoke the words

by rote, but as she did, she tried to imagine Jim standing where Nick stood.

And for the smallest moment, she wondered what might have been. Had Jim really changed into the man Nick thought he was? Did Jim really think of her as much as Nick said?

Would Kyle's presence in their lives have made a difference?

Nick touched the isolette, leaning closer to get a better look. "He is beautiful," he said quietly, his voice reverent. "I think he even looks a bit like Jim. Don't you think?"

Beth tried to see what Nick did. "I guess as a mother I just see *him*," was all she could say.

Nick gave her an odd look then smiled. "Of course." Then he shot a quick glance at the clock in the unit and Beth knew it was time to go.

Beth looked down at her baby, her heart sore. Though he was in excellent hands, the thought of leaving the hospital with empty arms cut her to the core. This was not how she had imagined the birth and delivery to be.

Then she looked across the isolette at Nick. He was watching her, a curious expression on his face. Of course in her imaginings she had never pictured a man like Nick bringing her back home. In her imaginings she was always alone.

The thought that Nick would bring her home gave her some small comfort.

"I suppose we should go," Beth said quietly.

Nick didn't say anything and Beth sensed he didn't want to rush her, but he stepped away to give her time with her baby.

Beth opened the isolette and bent over, brushing her lips over Kyle's soft cheek. He turned his button mouth toward her, seeking, and Beth's heart contracted.

"Bye, little one," she whispered, her voice breaking as tears threatened. She paused, swallowing. "See you in the morning." She waited, gathering her emotions as her little boy's head slipped to the side. He was asleep again.

"Is there really no place she can stay overnight in the hospital?" she heard Nick ask Kyle's nurse. He sounded upset.

"Unfortunately, the only way she can stay is if she's willing to sleep in this chair or in the lounge outside," the nurse replied, her voice even.

"That doesn't seem right."

"We can't accommodate every parent," the nurse replied. "It's just not practical or feasible."

Beth walked over to where Nick stood, his hands on his hips, a scowl pulling his dark eyebrows together as he glared at the nurse. He looked fierce and frightening.

"It's okay, Nick," Beth said, pulling her broken emotions back together, surprised at the controlled anger in his voice. "I'll be here in the morning." She had made sure they had a generous supply of milk for Kyle for night feedings. The nurse had helped her with that and told her they would make sure Kyle was well fed.

Nick glanced at her, his brows still furrowed. Curiously his anger over the situation gave her a warm feeling. It had been a long time since anyone had been concerned about her well-being and willing to go to bat for her.

"It's still not right," he grumbled, his scowl fading as he looked at her.

Beth glanced at the nurse who gave her a quick wink as if she understood exactly why Nick was so upset.

"You go home and get a good night's sleep, Beth," the nurse said with a warm smile. "If you feel the need to come anytime in the night, you just pop in. You know you can come 24/7 and stay as long as you want."

Beth knew she wouldn't be "popping in" anytime tonight or any night this week. Not with the ranch a good hour's drive from the hospital and no other place to stay in Calgary other than a hotel. "Thanks for letting me know, but I'll probably see you in the morning." Then she turned and left before the nurse could see the tears in her eyes.

She tried to brush them away without Nick seeing, but when she felt his hand on her shoulder, she knew he had.

"He's in good hands, you know," Nick said, his words oddly comforting.

"I know." Beth glanced over her shoulder at her baby, her heart constricting at the thought of leaving him. Then her gaze slipped to Nick.

For a moment she couldn't look away from his dark eyes. Didn't want to.

"Thanks for all your help," she said quietly, giving him a soft smile. "I really appreciate your support."

His answering smile kindled a gentle warmth in her soul. "I'm really thankful and humbled that I could be a part of this all." He released a short laugh. "I've seen so much sorrow..." his voice faded as he shrugged, but he kept his eyes on her. "It's just a real blessing to be a part of life at the beginning."

They held each other's gaze for a moment longer, sharing the moment, and as the connection lengthened, other emotions hovered in the silence between them.

Gratitude, appeal, attraction.

She shouldn't be doing this, Beth thought as she yanked off her protective gown and tossed it in the laundry bin. Hadn't being with Jim taught her anything about men?

Ellen waited for both of them in the lounge and when the doors slid open, she was on her feet, an expectant look on her face.

"How is my grandson doing?" she asked.

As she spoke, Beth was reminded of another moment, just this afternoon, when a nurse brought Bob into the unit.

He had come to the isolette and stared at Kyle, unashamed tears running down his face. It had made Beth both uncomfortable and uneasy. Through all of her planning she knew Bob and Ellen wouldn't be pleased with her plans.

She had just never considered their immediate attachment to Kyle.

"All things considered, he's doing really well," Beth said, trying to ignore Nick right behind her. "But he won't be able to come home for a bit yet."

Ellen took a step closer and then put her arm around Beth's shoulders. "Oh, honey, I wish I could do something for you." She gave Beth a quick hug, then waited, as if to see what Beth would do.

Beth wanted to lean into Ellen's embrace, to take the love her mother-in-law offered, but years of independence kept her from giving in to the impulse.

"Have you heard from your mother yet?" Ellen asked.

"Curt is bringing her tomorrow," Beth replied. "And how is Bob?"

"Seeing little Kyle had done him so much good. He apologizes, by the way, for being such a baby." Ellen shook her head as she smiled. "He told me he cried when he saw his grandson. Not often you get to see a cowboy cry."

Or a soldier.

Beth couldn't help a quick glance over her shoulder at Nick, thinking of his reaction to seeing Kyle.

He gave her a self-conscious grin, as if he understood exactly what she was thinking.

"We should get going. Bob wants me to check up on a few of the cows tonight," Nick said.

Half an hour later they were in the truck, making the last turn out of the city and leaving the lights of Calgary behind. Beth chose to sit in the backseat of the truck, preferring to keep her distance from Nick.

She didn't want the distraction of his presence. She had too many thoughts circling her mind, all demanding attention.

It was as if God was determined to keep her off balance. The plans she had laid out so carefully were scattered like papers in a storm. She no longer knew what she would do or what shape her life would take.

She did know she couldn't move to Vancouver until Kyle was much better. But could she stay on the ranch?

Her wayward thoughts flitted back to Bob sitting in his wheelchair by Kyle's isolette. The tears on his face had been a shock and a revelation to her.

Kyle was Ellen and Bob's son's child, and therefore he also belonged to them. In all her plans she had realized this on one level, but somehow had never absorbed it until she saw their reaction to him. Until she saw Bob's tears.

And she knew that no matter what her plans had been before, she had to consider Bob and Ellen now.

"How are you doing back there?" Ellen asked, turning around in her seat, her head a dark silhouette against the headlights of the truck lighting the road ahead.

"I'm fine. Tired."

"Do you know what time your mother is coming tomorrow?"

"I believe she said my brother was bringing her to the hospital at about noon."

"Will she be staying with you?"

Beth shook her head. "She's coming just for the day."

"So she's not staying to help you?"

"She's getting a ride with my brother and he has to be back tomorrow night."

"I could bring her back if you want her to stay," Nick said.

"That's very kind of you," Beth said quietly, wondering if her mother had even considered that option. "But I think my mother prefers not to change her plans."

"Well, if she does, the offer is still open."

Beth caught Nick looking at her in the rearview mirror, his eyes a dark smudge on his face. Once again she felt ensnared by his gaze and once again she forced herself to look away.

She rested her head back and closed her eyes. The busyness of the day and the tension of watching Kyle caught up to her. The fuzzy edges of sleep crept over her and her thoughts became a muddled mix of Kyle and the hospital.

But her last thought before sleep took over her mind was of Nick, looking at her across the isolette, his eyes bright with unshed tears.

"Beth. Beth, honey, time to wake up." Nick lightly shook Beth's shoulder, wishing he didn't have to wake her.

Ellen had already gone to the house, pleading exhaustion, and Nick said he would make sure Beth got home okay.

Beth's head lolled to one side, her hair, coming loose from its ponytail, sliding across her face. He brushed it aside, his fingers lingering over her cheek.

He couldn't help the hitch of his heart at the sight of her fragile features relaxed in sleep. She looked so innocent. He thought of the sorrow on her face when she had to leave her baby behind.

He wanted nothing more than to pull her into his arms, to protect her from more pain. Hadn't she had enough to deal with?

When he had taken Ellen to see Bob this afternoon, one of the first things she and Bob had done was pray out loud in the hospital room. They didn't seem to care that Nick was there, nor particularly mind. They prayed for Bob and they prayed for

Beth and they prayed for Kyle, and as Nick slipped out of the room to give them their privacy, he heard them mention his name, as well.

The thought gave him a feeling of comfort.

Praying together came so naturally to them, and their ease with God reminded Nick of his parents. How they had prayed together and taught him to pray.

As he looked down at Beth, he was envious of Bob and Ellen's devotion and wished he could so easily put the burdens he carried on God's shoulders.

He gave Beth another shake, trying to wake her, calling her name again.

She slowly lifted her head and her eyes drifted open. She blinked once, then again.

"Kyle," she said suddenly, struggling to undo her seat belt. "Where's Kyle? Where's my baby?"

Nick's heart broke for her as he recognized the sudden plunge from sleep into reality. The disorientation and the fear.

"It's okay, Beth," he said quietly, catching her hands in his and squeezing them. "He's safe. He's in the hospital. You're home. On the ranch."

Beth's eyes slowly lost the wild look and then she pulled her hands over her face, drawing in a shuddering breath.

"I had the most awful dream," she whispered, her voice breaking. "I dreamt I couldn't find Kyle anywhere. I dreamt I ran up and down the halls of the hospital and I could hear him crying but I couldn't find him."

The sorrow in Beth's voice cut Nick to the quick, and he gently undid her seat belt and drew her out of the backseat of the truck. Without thinking, he pulled her into his arms.

She rested her head against his chest, her erratic breathing slowing. But as he held her, his conscience accused him.

This isn't right. This is Jim's wife. He's only been dead a couple of months. You, of all people, have no right to hold her and comfort her.

But he couldn't let her go. Not when she seemed so lost, so alone. Not when she seemed to need him.

She clung to his arms, took another breath, then pulled away. "Thanks for being here," she said quietly. "And thanks for everything you've done for me."

Her eyes shone in the glow from the half-moon hanging above the mountains, and in the pale light, her face seemed luminous.

He gave her a smile, brushing a strand of hair

away from her face. He fought the urge to pull her close again, to lay a claim to her, but he couldn't.

"I did promise Jim I would watch over you," he said, forcing himself to bring Jim front and center.

It was as if someone had flicked off a light switch. Her eyes lowered and she pushed him away.

"Of course," she said. "Your promise to Jim."

Did he imagine the slightly bitter note in her voice? Where had that come from?

She reached behind her for her purse and slung it over her shoulder.

"I'll walk you back to the house," he said.

"You don't need to. I can manage on my own."

And with that she strode away from him, leaving him puzzled and confused as to the sudden change in her attitude.

Chapter Six

"So my grandson's not really sick or anything like that?" Tina Lassiter frowned as she sat back on the couch of the waiting room dedicated to the NICU and threaded her hands together. "He's going to be okay?"

"Beth already said he's going to be fine, Mom," Curt replied. "You don't need to worry."

"But all those monitors he's got attached to him, that can't be good." Tina chewed at her lower lip, her lined forehead puckered in worry. She had just come back from her visit with Kyle and had been fretting aloud ever since she returned to the waiting room.

Nick glanced from Tina Lassiter to Curt, Beth's brother, who sat beside his mother, his arm around her shoulder, the picture of the devoted son.

Curt and Beth's hair were the same color and

held the same curl. Tina had the same unique-colored eyes Beth had, but otherwise he couldn't see much resemblance between the people sitting across from Beth on the couch and Beth herself.

Beth spoke up. "The monitors are just a pre-caution—"

"What did the doctor tell you, Mom?" Curt asked, interrupting Beth. "He wouldn't say much to me."

"He did say that Kyle was very healthy." Tina gave Beth an encouraging smile. "That's good, isn't it? I mean, Beth doesn't need to have to worry about a sickly child, not with all she's got to think about." Tina sighed, then looked at Curt. "Can you get me a cup of tea, dear? I'm so thirsty."

"Of course." Curt got up and glanced from Nick to Beth to Ellen, who sat beside Beth. "Can I get anyone else anything? Nick? Ellen?"

"I'm good, thanks," Nick said, while Ellen just shook her head.

It wasn't until Curt left that Nick realized Curt hadn't asked Beth if she wanted anything to drink.

"Did you want something?" he asked her.

Beth glanced up at him, weariness etched in her features. "No. Thanks. I've been drinking water all day."

"Nick, I understand you were stationed in Afghanistan with Jim," Tina said, turning her attention to him. "I never understood what he did there. Maybe you could tell me?"

"I explained it to you, Mother," Beth said, a slightly defensive tone in her voice.

"I still have no idea," Tina said to Nick. "Maybe you can tell me, Nick."

Irritation flickered through Nick at Tina's distracted attitude toward Beth. He put it down to the tension of the moment. After all, it was Tina's grandchild that lay beyond the doors of the NICU, as well.

"Jim and I worked transport, NSE," Nick said. "We drove the HLVWs from KAF to the base."

"KAF is…"

"Sorry, Kandahar Airfield. And HLVW stands for Heavy Logistics Vehicle Wheeled, or essentially a heavy utility truck."

"You liked doing that?" Tina seemed puzzled. "You didn't mind not fighting like the rest of the soldiers?"

"Running the supply convoy outside the wire was often as dangerous as fighting. We've been hit almost as often as the troops we supplied. If we didn't run the convoy, the soldiers wouldn't have supplies to do their jobs, either. We played a critical role."

"So you saw heavy fighting?" Tina asked.

"Yeah. I saw some intense stuff."

"I understand you were with Jim when he died?" Tina commented.

"Yes. I was," he said, his words clipped. Nick glanced at Beth, gauging her reaction, wishing they didn't have to discuss this in front of her. She had enough to deal with right now and he wasn't eager to relive that day again.

"That's too bad." Tina looked at her entwined hands, then released a sigh. "Jim was a good man. A good husband." She looked up at Ellen. "You and Bob can be proud of how he served his country."

"We most certainly are," Ellen said quietly.

"Such a tragedy, though," Tina continued. "And so hard for our Beth, though she was always a little trooper herself," she said, granting Ellen a polite smile. "You know I wanted to say hello to you at the funeral, Ellen. Give you my condolences. I know it must have been hard for you. But it was such a difficult time for me. I…I'm not a widow like Beth, but I am alone. I don't know if Beth told you—she can be such a private person, always has been—but my husband left me fifteen years ago. It was a very, very hard time and it's in moments like Jim's funeral that I really feel how alone I am, so that's why I didn't talk to you."

"That's okay. I understand," Ellen said. An awkward pause followed Tina's admission, then Ellen glanced at Beth. "How are you doing, honey? Not too tired?"

"Beth doesn't tire that easily," Tina said with a quick laugh. "Like I said, trooper. Doesn't ask for help, either. I'm sure you had to drag her here once she found out she was in labor. Always was independent. She'd hide out, doing her own thing. Beth always liked to cut and glue and fiddle with paper," Tina said. "Made the cutest things. Always said she was going to be a card designer when she grew up. I tried to tell her she wouldn't get anywhere with that, so it's a good thing she married Jim." Tina gave Beth a quick wink.

Nick pressed back a yawn. He needed a break. He got to his feet and glanced at Beth. She sat, arms wrapped around herself, her eyes on the NICU doors as if hoping one of the nurses would ask her to come.

She looked tired and he didn't blame her. From the moment Beth's mother and brother arrived, they had talked nonstop. They seemed like very pleasant people, but the chitchat was wearing on him and he wondered if Beth felt the same.

Then she sent a fatigued look his way and he made a sudden decision.

"I'd like to see Kyle again, if that's okay," Nick said, raising his brows at Beth in question. He had held back, giving Beth's family time and space to see their grandson and nephew, but for now they seemed content to sit here in the lounge and visit.

Beth fairly leaped to her feet, a look of gratitude sweeping over her face. "I was just wondering how things are going with him, too." She turned to her mother. "Mom, I'm going to check on Kyle."

Her mother looked up at her and smiled. "Of course, honey. When Curt brings my tea I'll come and join you." Then Tina shot a frown at Nick. "Are you going with her?"

Her disapproval gave him pause.

I'm doing this for Beth, he reminded himself, dismissing the slightly jeering voice questioning his motives.

"I haven't seen Kyle today," he said quietly, holding Tina's gaze.

"Oh. I see." But Nick understood from her tone that she didn't.

"Shall we go?" Beth asked, standing by the door.

Nick nodded. As they donned protective gowns,

Beth glanced over at Nick. "I hope you aren't too offended by my mother's last comment."

Nick frowned, pretending not to understand.

"Sometimes she can pack a lot in only three words," Beth said.

Nick gave her an encouraging smile as he slipped his gown over his clothes. "Don't worry about it. I've endured a whole lot more than disapproving mothers. At least she cares."

Beth shot him a relieved look. "Thanks for understanding."

"I can see how the situation might look to her," he continued. "A single guy hanging around a recently widowed woman. Could seem a bit weird."

Beth tied up her gown then glanced over at him. "It's not weird to me."

Nick paused, trying to figure out what she was saying.

"I can't tell you how much I appreciate you being here for me now," she added. "Driving me back and forth to the hospital. Helping out Bob and Ellen like you are." She looked up at him, her gaze steady. "You being here helps. A lot. Thank you."

Nick felt an odd emotion stirring and shifting in his chest as he looked into her violet eyes. "You're welcome." He held back a comment about doing this for Jim because he knew that wouldn't be true.

His being here with Beth right now had nothing to do with Jim. And everything to do with her.

She flashed him a shy smile, then walked ahead of him. At the doorway to the pod, she faltered and reached out.

"Beth. What's wrong?" Nick was immediately at her side, holding her up. Again.

She blinked and looked dazedly around, still holding on to the doorway. "I feel kind of strange," she said. "Dizzy."

"Let me bring you back to the lounge," Nick insisted, his arm around her waist.

She took a long, deep breath, then pushed herself away from the doorway. "It's gone. I just felt a bit light-headed."

"Do you need something to eat? To drink?" Nick asked, suddenly concerned.

She waved him off. "No. It's gone. Maybe I just moved too fast." Then she looked away from him, her hand pressed to her chest in alarm. "What is Kyle's doctor doing here? He did rounds this morning."

Beth hurried toward Kyle's bed but Nick stayed

right beside her to make sure she didn't falter again.

Kyle's doctor stood at the station, frowning at Kyle's chart, his glasses perched up on his forehead.

"Is something wrong, Doctor Rudmik?" Beth's voice held a thread of panic and Nick had to hold back his own anxiety.

Doctor Rudmik looked up and when he saw Beth the frown slipped away, replaced with a smile as he slipped his glasses onto his nose. "Your little guy is doing great. He's gaining weight and his Apgar scores are good. In fact, he's doing so well, I think we'll let Kyle go home tomorrow."

Beth sagged with relief and Nick came behind her, holding her up. Her hand rested on her chest and her face showed clearly the strain of the past few days.

"Tomorrow?"

"Unless you want us to keep him," the doctor said with a grin.

"No, of course not," Beth said, her voice breaking. "I'm so glad. Thank you, Doctor Rudmik."

The doctor nodded and Nick sensed that he was just as glad to be delivering the news as Beth was to receive it. He gave her a quick smile. "Your little boy is a fighter. He's doing well. He's got a few mucous issues so you'll have to watch for that. I'll get the nurse to write up some instructions and give you some information on anything else you might want to be vigilant about."

Beth nodded as if she understood, but Nick sensed her entire attention was on Kyle.

Doctor Rudmik seemed to recognize that as well and looked to Nick.

"We'll make sure it gets done," Nick said.

Doctor Rudmik nodded, made another note on Kyle's chart, then slipped it in the holder. "He'll be fine, Beth." Then he left.

Beth lifted the lid of the isolette and picked up her baby. "Just one more night in the hospital, little guy, and then you can come home. And you can stay right next to me and I don't have to come here to visit you." Beth eased herself into the chair beside the isolette and, maneuvering herself around the wires attached to her son, drew Kyle close to her, her eyes alight with wonder as she murmured quietly to her baby. The serenity of her expression touched Nick in a way that nothing had before.

Nick tried to hold the moment, sensing that this was a side of Beth not many people saw.

Beth nuzzled Kyle's cheeks, a look of utter bliss on her features. It was as if she finally dared believe Kyle would make it.

She looked up at Nick and the smile she gave him was so open, so carefree and dazzling, it made his heart stutter in reaction.

Then he couldn't stop himself. He reached up and cupped Beth's face. Caressed her cheek.

She held his gaze for a long moment, then Kyle stirred, waved his arms and began to cry.

The sound broke the moment and Nick jerked his hand back, pushing aside the fanciful thoughts.

What had he done? He had no right to be here. This was Jim's place. It was supposed to be Jim that Beth looked up at with such peace and joy.

He gave her a tight smile in return, then limped away, as if to give her privacy to take care of her son.

He jerked his gown off at the entrance, pausing a moment to catch his equilibrium. When Bob was well enough to manage the ranch, Nick had to leave.

A tiny thought crept around the edges of his consciousness. Could he? Should he?

He shook his head, as if to pull himself back to the present. He rubbed a dollop of hand sanitizer over his hands, then went through the doors.

Tina looked up when Nick joined them. "Should I go in?"

"Beth is just feeding the baby," Nick said. He

wanted to tell them the news about Kyle, but that wasn't his news to pass on.

"Nick, Ellen tells me you are on leave from the army," Tina said. "You won't be going back?"

Nick nodded, still trying to find his footing after that moment with Beth.

"I'm curious what brings you here. To this area," Tina said.

What should he tell her? He scratched his forehead, trying to find the right way to explain what he was doing here.

"As you know, Nick was with Jim when he died," Ellen answered, saving him from having to explain. "And Jim made him promise he would come to the ranch to see us." Ellen shot Nick a quick look. "And I suspect Jim also asked Nick to deliver a last message to Beth and to make sure Beth was okay."

Some kind of job he was doing with that, Nick thought with a stab of guilt.

"That's admirable," Tina said quietly. "I'm sure you must have your own struggles with coming back here."

You have no idea, Nick thought. "It's an adjustment."

"How does your family feel about your service?"

Tina asked. "I'm sure they must be proud of what you've done."

"I was an only child. My parents died when I was eighteen."

"Really? How?" Tina asked.

"Car accident," he said, wishing he didn't sound so curt. Tina was simply being curious.

"Oh, my goodness. That's so sad. But unfortunately, there's so many bad drivers on the road you have to be so careful." Tina held her hand up. "Not that I'm saying your father was a bad driver. I'm sure he was very careful."

"He was." Nick jumped to his feet. "I'm going downstairs. Get a breath of fresh air. Just call me on my cell phone when you're ready to go," he said to Ellen and Bob.

"If you're leaving anyway, can you bring me back to my room?" Bob asked. "I've got to go to physio in half an hour and I want to rest before I go."

"Oh, honey, I'm so sorry," Ellen said, making a move to get up. "I forgot."

Bob gave her a forgiving smile and reached out and squeezed her hand. "Don't you worry about me. You just stay and keep Tina and Curt company. I'll be fine."

"When can you go home, Bob?" Tina asked.

"Doctor will tell me tomorrow," Bob said, shooting Nick a pleading glance.

Nick grinned as he walked over to Bob's wheelchair. He understood exactly what Bob was asking him.

"If I don't see you before you have to leave, I hope you have a safe trip back home," Nick said to Tina. "It was nice to meet you and Curt."

Tina gave him an odd look and nodded. "Nice to meet you, too."

Nick grabbed the handles of Bob's wheelchair and hurried out of the waiting room.

"Trying to win some kind of wheelchair derby?" Bob asked, shooting Nick a wry glance.

"Nope. Just making a quick getaway."

Bob chuckled, then sucked in a quick breath. Nick slowed down the pace. "Sorry about that."

"Nothing you did, Nick. Just pain." Bob sighed. "Of course I'd sooner deal with this than listen to that woman all afternoon. Poor Ellen. I feel like I'm abandoning her."

Nick felt the same.

"Now I understand why Beth's so quiet. Poor kid probably never had a chance to get a word in edgewise with her mother and her brother around. And that was only one of the brothers."

Nick let Bob's observation settle into his mind.

He thought of how Beth talked to Kyle, how her words seemed to pour out of her.

Bob shifted in his wheelchair again.

"You feeling okay?" Nick asked, concerned.

"It hurts a lot, but what bothers me more is that I'm depending on you to help out." He looked back at Nick. "You don't have to stay at the ranch, you know. I could see if my neighbors would help out. I'm sure you've got plans."

Nick looked down at Bob, then away, thinking of how he had resisted being here. How he had initially wanted to leave and how that had temporarily changed.

"I don't have that many plans," Nick replied as he maneuvered Bob's wheelchair into an elevator. "I'm just winging it anyway and, like I said, I'm only too glad to help you out. It's a way of…a way of repaying a debt."

"What debt?" Bob shot him a puzzled frown. "What could you possibly owe us?"

Nick tightened his grip on the handles of the wheelchair. "More than you can know," he said quietly.

He knew he hadn't answered Bob's question, but he wasn't ready to.

He couldn't face that dark place yet.

Chapter Seven

Could she really do this? Could she really take care of this tiny, helpless child?

Beth looked up from Kyle and glanced around the room she had been moved to in Bob and Ellen's house, a mixture of emotions running through her.

Happiness to be away from the hospital. Fear at being responsible for Kyle. Wondering if she should have agreed to move into the big house with Ellen and Bob.

And Nick.

Then another wave of dizziness washed over her and she recognized this was the right thing to do. She held Kyle a little closer as she sat in the rocking chair beside the crib.

"I'm thankful you decided to come and stay at the house." Ellen fussed over the crib she and

Nick had set up while Beth was in the hospital. "I know how independent you are, but I am glad you decided to listen to the doctor."

Yesterday, after her mother had left, Beth had another dizzy spell. This time one of the nurses was around. Her doctor had examined her and told her she had lost more blood than he realized and she would have to take it very easy for another week.

When Ellen found out, she insisted, along with Nick, that Beth move into the main house.

"Are you sure this isn't too much for you?" Beth asked one more time, still unsure of the setup. Being in the house meant she was closer to Nick.

And after that moment of connection in the hospital yesterday, she wasn't sure that was a good idea.

"Nonsense," Ellen said with an unladylike snort. "You're my daughter-in-law and if your mother could stay, it wouldn't be too much for her, either."

"But Bob needs you." Beth felt she had to lodge one more protest.

Ellen waved that off, as well. "Nick said he'd gladly help out as long as he's needed. And if Nick can't, we have neighbors. I couldn't forgive myself if something happened to you while you were all alone in that other house."

"Just until I'm feeling better, okay?" Beth insisted.

Ellen gave her a gentle smile. "We'll take it one day at a time, my dear."

Beth sat back in the chair, feeling much better. One day at a time was how she had lived her life for the past few months. She could do it a little longer.

"So, you're settled in for the night? You've got everything you need?" Ellen asked, tugging at the quilt, adjusting the mobile above the crib.

Beth looked from the little table beside her chair, complete with a pitcher of water and a cup, to the crib and stocked changing table, to the bed along one wall for her. Ellen had thought of everything. "This is perfect."

"All right, then," Ellen said. "I hope you can sleep tonight. I'll be sleeping a lot better just knowing you're only a few steps away." She hesitated and Beth sensed she wanted to say something more. "If you don't mind, there's one thing I want to do with you before I go," Ellen said, coming to Beth's side and kneeling down on the carpet beside the chair, her hand cradling Kyle's head. "If it's okay, I'd like to pray with you."

Beth didn't see that coming and wasn't sure how to respond.

"I know you don't come to church with us, but I also know from talking to your mother that you were also raised as a Christian." Ellen looked down at Kyle and sighed lightly. "I am so thankful things went well and I want to acknowledge that. With you."

An unexpected wave of emotion washed over Beth. She hadn't prayed for years. Not since her father left. Not since her mother fell into her own well of grief as a result of her father's abandonment and stopped paying attention to her. Not since she realized that she was on her own.

But she could hardly deny what Ellen wanted. She was in Ellen's house and she knew that Bob and Ellen had a strong and basic faith in God. Just because she didn't share that faith, didn't mean she couldn't let Ellen pray.

"That will be fine," Beth said quietly.

Ellen kept her one hand on Kyle's tiny head, almost dwarfing it, then she wove her other hand through Beth's and bowed her head. Beth followed suit.

"Dear Lord, thank You so much for this precious gift of life," Ellen prayed, her voice melodious. "Thank You for Beth, and we pray she may feel better and stronger soon. Thank You that Kyle and Beth could be here for a while, thank You for the gift they are to Bob and I. I pray You will be a light to them in their darkness and a comfort to them in their loneliness, as You are a comfort to Bob and I." Ellen paused, as if thinking of her own loss, and Beth squeezed her hand tighter, conveying her own sorrow and sympathy to her mother-in-law. "Bless and watch over Bob in the hospital and I pray that we may all be together again soon. Amen."

A gentle silence followed Ellen's prayer and for a moment it was as if a voice whispered across Beth's mind. A voice she hadn't heard in years.

I love you.

Beth pressed her lips together, her head still bent, a light shiver trickling down her spine.

Then Ellen squeezed her hand again and slowly got to her feet and the moment faded away.

Beth kept her attention on Kyle, blinking away unexpected tears. "Thank you for that," she said quietly.

Then, to her surprise, she felt the light brush of Ellen's kiss over her head. "You're welcome, my dear. I hope you sleep well."

Then, without another word, Ellen left, closing the door behind her with a quiet click.

Beth looked at her little boy, still sleeping in her

arms. He lay with his head to one side, his mouth pursed, one hand curled up against his cheek.

So innocent. So precious.

I love you.

The echo of the disembodied voice raised a tendril of anger, a ghost of past pain.

Do You? she challenged, questions tumbling through her mind, each crying out to be voiced. *Do You really love me? If You do, then why have things turned out the way they have? Why did my father leave? Why did my mother retreat so far into herself that she forgot she had a daughter? Why did Jim end up being such an unfaithful husband and why did You let me endure the humiliation of my marriage?*

The questions reverberated through her mind, doubling back on themselves, spinning around in her head, growing stronger and more forceful, feeding the flames of her anger.

If You love me, why am I all alone, a widow with a baby to raise?

You're not alone.

The words sifted through her questions, separating and dividing them, breaking them down.

You're not alone.

The words settled into her mind as she breathed in the delicate, almost spicy scent of her newborn son, as she brushed her cheek over his impossibly soft skin, his downy hair.

She wasn't alone, now, she admitted. Not with her little boy in her arms. Not with Ellen down the hall.

You're not alone.

A gentle knock on the door pulled her out of the endless cycle of thoughts.

"Come in," she said quietly, so as not to wake Kyle.

Nick ducked his head into the room, smiling when he saw her.

"I saw the light on in your room when I came back from feeding the cows, so I thought I would check on you."

It was on the tip of her tongue to tell him that Ellen already had, but the thought that he was watching her gave her a peculiar comfort.

You are not alone.

"I'm just about to go to bed," she said.

"That's good. You look exhausted."

"Oh, I bet you say that to all the ladies," she said, clinging to flippancy to keep her previous thoughts at bay.

Nick grinned. "No. Only the ones that look exhausted." He came a little farther into the room, but stayed by the door.

His hesitancy puzzled her. Yesterday, when they were in the hospital, when he touched her cheek, she felt something building between them.

But since then he had kept his distance and she had reprimanded herself for her overactive imagination.

Beth got up and gently laid Kyle in the crib. He looked lost in it. She tucked the flannel sheet a bit tighter around him, then pulled the quilt on top of him. Kyle coughed, then sputtered, his hands waving as he fought for breath.

Beth snatched him up.

"Is he breathing? Is he okay?" Beth cried out.

Nick was instantly at her side, bending over to look more closely at Kyle. Then he straightened with a smile. "Yes. He's breathing."

"I don't hear anything."

Nick gently took him from her. "Here, put your ear by his mouth."

Beth did and heard the reassuring sound of Kyle's breathing and her heart slowed.

"Thank goodness. The doctor said I had to watch for mucous, but I thought he just meant a runny nose." Beth took Kyle from Nick, held him close and drew in a long, slow breath as another wave of dizziness washed over her. Black spots danced in front of her eyes and she swayed.

And once again, Nick caught her.

"Seriously, Beth. You've got to go to bed."

She wanted to wave him off, but his arm around her waist was comforting. "I will."

Nick gently took Kyle away from her, laid him down in the crib and pulled the blanket over his body.

Then he helped Beth to the bed. She was about to reach down to take off her slippers, but he was already bending over and pulling them off her feet, his hands so gentle she felt like sighing.

Beth looked down at Nick's bent head, his dark hair with its gentle curl. Her heart stuttered and she had to fight the urge to touch his head, to let her fingers linger on his hair.

She felt a yearning so deep it almost hurt.

You're a widow. Jim's only been gone a few months. How can you be thinking about any man—about Nick—that way?

But Jim never loved me. He never cared for me the way Nick has been.

You're alone. Always have been. Always will be. You can't depend on anyone. No one cares. You're on your own.

But in spite of the conflicting voices in her head, her hand lifted toward Nick.

Then Nick was standing and pulling the blankets back for her and she quickly lowered her arm.

"Into bed now, missy," he said quietly.

"Thanks for your help," she said, trying to pull herself together as she slid beneath the covers, exhaustion clouding her thoughts. "You're a good man."

Nick looked down at her, a peculiar expression moving over his face. "Don't believe that," he said, his voice suddenly grim.

Beth didn't have the energy to ask him what he meant by that. She just murmured a good-night, then let herself slip into a deep, dreamless sleep.

Jim's wife. She's Jim's wife.
And Jim is dead.

Nick jumped out of the tractor, his thoughts fighting with each other. Checking up on Beth last night had been a mistake. Once again he'd ended up too close to her. He had no right to do that.

He pulled out a knife and hacked at the plastic twine, holding the hay bale tight as if taking out his frustration on the strings.

He had agreed to help Bob out and there was no way he could back out of that now. Not with Bob barely mobile. Ellen had her hands full taking care of her husband and Beth and the baby. She needed him, as well.

And Beth?

Nick sighed as he wound the strings up into a tight bundle. He hadn't figured on staying this long in spite of what he had promised Jim.

But staying around Beth was getting to be dangerous.

He'd listened to so many stories about Beth from Jim, seen enough pictures of her that he had fallen half in love with her before he even met her.

Last night, when he came in the room and saw her nuzzling her baby, the pale light of the table lamp casting her face in shadows, creating a picture that could have been a painting of *Madonna and Child*, he'd felt a perfect storm of conflicting emotions.

He wanted to protect her. He wanted to take care of her.

But he wasn't the right person for that.

He turned up the collar of his coat around his neck against the wind that had started up with the past half hour. He shot a glance at the mountains, watching the clouds scatter over their peaks. Maybe a storm coming in.

"Hey, Nick."

As if his thoughts had called her to him, he heard Beth's voice.

He looked around and saw her walking toward

the fence, tugging a toque tighter over her ears. She wore an oversize jacket and from the way the coat curved, he guessed Kyle was bundled close to her underneath the coat.

"Hey, yourself," he returned, hesitating. What was she doing out and about already? She just about fainted last night.

Then he fought his better sense and walked toward the fence.

"I thought I would take Kyle out for a breath of fresh air."

Nick glanced down at her hand, resting lightly on the mound under her coat, and he imagined Kyle nestled against her chest, cozy and warm and sheltered.

"You're not feeling too dizzy?"

Beth gave him a gentle smile and shook her head. "I had a really good sleep. Ellen gave me a huge breakfast and I wanted so badly to get out."

"It's kind of cold out today."

"I'm dressed warm," she said.

He pulled his gaze and his thoughts away from her, up at the sky. The sky was a molten gray and now and then the wind would gust.

"Don't go too far. There's a storm coming in."

"I won't," was all she said. He was about to go

back to his work when she spoke again. "Ellen told me you're moving into my old house."

"Yeah. I just figured Ellen had enough going on. She didn't need me underfoot." And he wasn't sure staying under the same roof as Beth was such a good idea, either. "I'm just sleeping on the couch."

"Don't do that. The couch is so lumpy and old. I don't mind if you use the bed."

Jim's old bed. Probably not a good idea. He had enough ghosts of Jim floating through his head.

He jerked his thumb toward the cows. "Sorry. I got the tractor running. I want to get the cows fed before the snow comes in."

A look of hurt crossed her face and while he regretted putting it there, keeping her at a distance was the smartest choice. When it was time to go, it had to be with his emotions untouched, his heart intact.

It was the only way to survive.

Chapter Eight

Beth watched Nick stride back to the tractor, puzzlement vying with relief.

Though she had fallen immediately asleep last night after Nick had left, she'd had enough time to relive those few moments with Nick each time Kyle woke up during the night for a feeding.

It had been hard not to forget how gentle and considerate he was. So when she thought of seeing Nick this morning her heart fluttered in anticipation.

But he hadn't been downstairs. When Ellen had told her he was out feeding the cows, Beth suddenly had an urge to take Kyle for a walk, thinking she might see Nick.

Except he didn't seem inclined to talk to her.

She thought they had shared something, but obviously it was just her overactive imagination and the loneliness that gripped her from time to time.

Beth cradled her arms around Kyle as if sheltering him, then walked slowly down the driveway, keeping the wind at her back. She was still a bit unsteady on her feet and it was chilly outside, but she needed to get out of Ellen's house. Though Ellen was kind and considerate of Beth's privacy, Beth still felt a nagging discomfort staying there.

She cast a longing look at her own little house. "What do you think, Kyle?" she asked her son, stroking his tiny body through the layers of the coat and baby carrier that Ellen had found for her. "Should I go and work on some new cards? I don't have a reason to make more but it would be fun to try to make some baby cards. Work with some softer colors."

She began down the driveway. "See, I could make a card for you. A Welcome to the World, Kyle card. You might not appreciate it now, but maybe someday. Or, better yet, I could start making a little photo book for you." She smiled at the thought. She had always made cards but she had so many supplies that the shift from card-making to scrapbooking would be a natural transition. "I could use chipboard and cover it. Shellie has a machine I can use to punch the pages and bind them. I'd have to get pictures of you. I can use that digital camera I haven't unpacked yet."

The camera had been Jim's going-away-slash-apology present before he was deployed to Afghanistan. He'd given it to her one week before he left. The camera was so she could take pictures and email them to him.

That had been the plan until Beth found the text messages on the cell phone Jim had left behind. Text messages from someone who called herself Toots. Who said she would miss Jim and think of him all the time and count the days until they could be back together again.

Beth had never sent Jim a text message in all their married life. And she had certainly never called herself Toots.

So Beth never took pictures and never sent any in an email. But the camera was still around. She could use it now.

The camera wasn't in her card room. She checked a number of boxes then stopped as she remembered.

The camera was in Jim's truck.

So she walked around the house to the garage at the back. The truck wasn't locked and sure enough, there it was in the glove box in the case Jim had bought for her.

She took the case out and glanced down at it, trying to examine how she felt as she held Jim's last gift. Sometimes her largest emotion was relief. But whenever Nick talked about Jim and how he loved her, tiny hope flickered deep in her heart. A hope that the text messages could be explained. A tiny, fragile hope that she had nurtured the past two times Jim had cheated on her.

She extinguished that hope. She shouldn't be so foolish. She tucked the camera in her pocket, but by now, after even the little bit of work she had done, she was sweating profusely. Kyle, thankfully, was still asleep. She caught her breath, her hand resting on the side of Jim's truck. It sounded as if someone was calling her name.

She paused, listening.

"Beth. Beth. Where are you?" She heard Nick's voice calling out across the yard. He sounded upset.

What was wrong? Had something happened to Ellen? Beth quickened her pace. Then stopped when she felt a jolt of pain through her midsection. No running for a while, obviously.

Then she came around the copse of trees separating the main house from her house and she saw Nick running down the driveway, the hitch in his gait more pronounced.

"Beth," she heard him call out again. He sounded panicked.

"Nick. I'm here. What's wrong?" she called out.

He skidded to a halt, spun around, then when he saw her, he changed direction. Even from here Beth saw the anger on his face. What had happened?

"Where were you?" he called out as he came closer.

Beth slowed down, puzzled at his anger. "I just went to get my camera from Jim's truck."

He stopped in front of her, his eyes blazing. She wasn't sure what she saw in their icy depths, but it gave her a frisson of fear. "You should have told Ellen or me," he said.

Beth frowned in puzzlement. "I wasn't gone long—"

"Ellen thought you went down the driveway, then she couldn't see you and she checked the house and you weren't there. She was frantic with worry."

Ellen charged out of Beth's house, her open coat flying out behind her. "Beth. Thank the good Lord, there you are. Where were you?"

Beth glanced from Nick to Ellen, puzzled at their worry and at Nick's anger. "I'm sorry. I just went to get my camera from Jim's truck." She wasn't used to this. She'd always gone her own way when she lived at home. Her mother never cared that much where she was, her brothers even less.

And Jim? After their first year of marriage, he couldn't be bothered to care.

Ellen's shoulders sagged with relief. "Oh, honey. I thought for sure something terrible had happened to you and Kyle."

Nick didn't say anything, but in his eyes Beth caught a glimpse of the same emotions she'd seen in them that moment they shared in the hospital when he cupped her cheek.

And last night.

He cares more than he lets on.

The thought curled around her heart and, surprisingly, kindled a gentle warmth.

"Sorry if we scared you," Nick muttered. "We were just worried."

In spite of the chilly wind swirling around her, the warmth grew in Beth's soul. It had been years since anyone worried about her, since anyone had gone running after her.

"That's okay," she said, still holding his gaze as the ice in his eyes melted away, replaced by a shimmering awareness.

She felt an answering lilt in her heart.

She blinked, then reluctantly pulled her gaze

away. "Next time I'll let you know exactly what I'm up to."

"That would be nice." Ellen gave her a one-armed hug. "Well, you better come back to the house. It's not very nice out right now. I was looking for you to say goodbye."

Beth frowned. "Where are you going? Bob doesn't come home until Monday, tomorrow."

"I'm going to church and then after that, to Calgary. I didn't want to drive back and forth in one day so I'm staying at my sister's place tonight. She lives in Bragg Creek."

"I still think you should let me drive you," Nick said.

"To church?" Ellen raised a questioning eyebrow and when Nick didn't answer, she smiled.

Beth felt a moment of guilt. Should she go to church, too? She hadn't in months.

"Don't worry, you two. I'd love it if you came to church with me, but I prefer that you attend because you want to." She smiled at Beth. "Besides, I'm going for lunch with a friend after church. If I don't feel comfortable driving to Calgary, she said she and her husband would bring me, as well."

Ellen gave Beth another one-armed hug. "I'm glad you're okay and I just wanted to say goodbye."

Beth nodded, trying not to think of the implications of Ellen's departure.

She and Nick would be alone on the ranch tonight.

Nick pulled his collar up against the snow driving down from the mountain.

Cows were bedded for the night. Ellen had left ten minutes ago with promises she would call when she got to Calgary.

And Beth?

Nick shot a quick glance over at the main house and through the driving snow saw lights on downstairs. In spite of his and Ellen's initial scare, Beth looked fine this afternoon. She was probably fine now. No need to go over and check.

He shivered, then ducked his head against the blinding snow and followed the path to the darkened house, wishing yet again that Ellen had let him drive her to Calgary. But she was insistent and he couldn't very well force the issue.

He went directly to the kitchen and heated up the leftover stew Ellen had brought over this afternoon. When that was done, he took the bowl and a slice of Ellen's homemade bread to the living room.

He dropped onto the lumpy couch and turned on the television while he ate with one hand, flipping through the channels with the other.

The stew was delicious, the bread heavenly, but supper only took up ten minutes of the evening.

He pushed himself up from the couch and wandered to the window again, looking through the darkness to the lights of the main house he could barely see through the trees.

She's fine and she probably doesn't want you there, he reminded himself, then turned around, looking around the living room. No magazines. A few books.

What did Beth do here all evening by herself?

He glanced back at the television set but the programs didn't interest him. He glanced up the stairs. Beth had told him he could sleep in her former room. Maybe he should check it out.

But when he stood in the doorway of the bedroom, all he could think was "Jim had slept here."

He spun around and was about to go back downstairs when he saw the door ajar to another room. Maybe there was a bed there he could sleep on.

He pushed the door open and flicked on the light switch. A desk stood against one wall, a cart of file folders beside it. On the other side was another table covered with small jars, boxes, ribbon, paper and some strange-looking machine plugged into the wall.

Curious, he walked to the desk and picked up a card he guessed Beth had made. It was bright and cheery with colorful pieces of paper decorating it and a ribbon along the bottom.

He opened the card but it was blank inside.

He put it down and saw another which made him smile. The back of the card was red polka dots and what looked like a pocket of a pair of blue jeans was pasted on top of that with some red hearts peeking out of the pocket. String and heart-shaped buttons finished off the side of the card. Underneath was written, "Wishing you a pocket full of love."

He smiled as he opened the card. Again, the inside was blank. Had this one been meant for Jim? As he laid the card down, Nick couldn't remember Jim ever getting a card from Beth. Jim freely shared his mail with Nick. At night, he read every letter he got from his parents out loud to Jim.

But never anything from Beth, which surprised Nick considering the amount of cards stacked up on her table.

He picked up another one that had a simple "Thank You" written out on a piece of paper layered over another piece of paper which was tied with a ribbon. Looked like a lot of work and paper just to thank someone.

Inside the card said:

To Bob and Ellen. I wish I could find exactly the right words to tell you how much your love and support have meant to me. You opened your home and your heart and I don't know how else to thank you. Except by way of this card. You are a blessing to me and my future child. Thank you.

Beth's name, in elegant script, was written at the bottom of the sentiment. Obviously this card had been made before Beth went into the hospital and hadn't been delivered yet.

Nick closed the card, feeling as if he had transgressed on something personal. He thought of the card tacked to Bob and Ellen's refrigerator and he wondered if Beth had written such personal words inside it, as well.

He closed the card, tracing the raised goldembossed flourish that framed the paper on the front of the card.

The ringing of the phone broke into the quiet.

He dropped the card and picked up the telephone sitting on Beth's desk.

"Nick. Please, come to the main house now. It's Kyle. Something's wrong."

Chapter Nine

Beth paced in front of the window as the wind howled around the building, tossing snow against the windows, taunting Beth's helplessness.

She clutched her son, hoping, praying Nick would come quick.

Kyle tried to pull in another breath, his tiny mouth working as he gasped for air. Should she call 911?

Would the ambulance be able to come in this storm?

The front door burst open and Nick flew in, his jacket open, the laces of his boots untied. He kicked them off and ran toward Beth, the hitch in his step not slowing him down one iota.

"What's happening?" Nick held out his hands for Kyle.

"Something's wrong." Beth laid Kyle in Nick's

arms. Nick held him away from him, Kyle's tiny head dwarfed by Nick's capable hands.

"He's choking," Nick said, his voice grim. He tipped Kyle over onto his arm, supporting his head with his hand. He thumped his back a couple of times with the heel of his hand, then turned him over. But Kyle's little mouth was still working like a little fish, trying to breathe.

"When did you notice this?" Nick asked while he turned him over and repeated the motion.

"Just before I called you. I was holding him and he coughed and then he started to have a hard time breathing."

"Probably mucous," Nick muttered, turning Kyle over again. "Get me a turkey baster."

Beth didn't stop to ask why. She fled to the kitchen. Her heart raced and she couldn't seem to control her hands as she searched through Ellen's drawers.

She found two basters. One small, one large. She grabbed them both and ran back to the living room, her heart pounding so hard it almost choked her.

Nick was pressing on Kyle's chest with two fingers.

Nick grabbed the smaller turkey baster, laid Kyle

on his side and worked it into his mouth. Then he suctioned.

Beth's trembling knees gave way and she dropped to the couch. Half-formed prayers swirled through her mind.

Please, Lord. Please.

Nick turned Kyle over, thumped his chest again, then suctioned again.

Then, amazingly, Kyle coughed and pulled in a huge breath.

And then started to cry.

Nick slipped to his knees on the floor and gently turned Kyle upward, holding him close.

"Thank You, Lord," Beth heard him say as he rocked her son, his eyes closed. "Thank You, Lord."

Beth wrapped her arms around herself, tremors of relief wracking her body. She added her silent thanks as she dropped to the floor beside Nick.

Nick drew in a shaky breath, still rocking Kyle, whose cries had faded to whimpers.

She reached for her son and Nick reluctantly released him into her care. Beth held Kyle away from her, making sure he was breathing. His cheeks were pink, his eyes closed, and Beth drew in another shaky breath.

"Thank you, Nick," was all she could say, her

voice a mere whisper. "Thank you. I don't know what I would have done if something had happened to him."

She held Kyle close to her, her eyes closed as she drew in a ragged breath.

"Is he breathing normally?" Nick asked, his voice tense.

Beth felt the tiny puffs of air coming from her baby's mouth against her neck and nodded.

Relief slivered through her, sucking strength from her arms and legs.

"I didn't know what to do," she whispered, rocking her son. "I was so scared. He was having such a hard time breathing and I thought even if I call the ambulance it would take too long to come here." The words spilled out of her, falling over each other. "I'm so glad you came. Thank you."

Nick shook his head. "You don't have to thank me."

"But I do. I need to say it." Her voice broke as she spoke. She swallowed down the sob that jumped into her throat. No. She couldn't let herself cry.

Nick stroked her back, his touch welcome and comforting. "Everything is okay now. Kyle's okay." Nick's quiet voice, his warm hand on her back, soothed her fears away, but with that came reaction.

"I was so scared. I was praying and praying…" A sob broke her voice. Then, against her will, the first few tears spilled. First a trickle, a gentle slide of moisture down her cheeks. Then she drew in another shaking breath and her body shuddered.

She tried to hold back the sorrow, but it was as if the first few tears were a crack in a dam and the pressure became too much to hold back.

She fought against it. She couldn't let go. The storm of emotion would overtake her and where would she be? She had to hold it together for the sake of her sanity.

For the sake of her son. She had to be strong for Kyle.

Then she felt Nick slip his arms around her and pull her to him, sheltering her. His arms created a sanctuary, giving her permission to be weak.

As she leaned against him, Beth's tears rose up from a place of deep pain, coming in waves, battering the defenses she had put in place and shored up over the years.

Her tears flowed for her son, growing up without a father, for Bob and Ellen who had lost so much, for her marriage that had been broken from the day it started. She cried for lost dreams of the past and the bleakness of a lonely future. She cried for the loss of her faith and the losses in her life. All the pain she had always pushed down, held back, kept hidden.

The pain she couldn't express because she didn't have anyone to hold her up.

As her heart released years of sorrow, she felt Nick's arms holding her and Kyle, rocking her, murmuring words of comfort and encouragement that registered on one part of her consciousness. Words that wound themselves around her battered, weary soul.

Slowly the storm subsided and her tears dried. She lay against Nick, unwilling to leave the sanctuary of his arms as her eyes burned and her head ached.

Nick's hand rested on her head, his fingers tangled in her hair. His cheek lay against her forehead and his whiskers rasped against her skin. His arms, strong and capable, held her against his chest and beneath the rough fabric of his shirt, now damp with her tears, she felt the steady, solid beat of his heart.

"It's okay," Nick whispered into her hair, his deep voice soothing as he stroked her arm with his other hand. "Everything is going to be okay."

For that moment, for this space in time, she

believed him. For the first time in years she believed "okay" was a possibility in her life.

Kyle stirred again, releasing a gentle sigh as if reminding Beth that she had other obligations.

She reluctantly pulled away from Nick. She looked down at the dark spot on Nick's shirt, evidence of her tears, and touched it gently.

"I'm sorry," she said, her voice quiet.

Nick cupped her cheek and turned her face up to his. "You have nothing to apologize for," he said, his thumb gently stroking her chin.

She nodded her agreement. Then, before she could stop herself, her hand brushed his cheek, a mere whisper of a touch.

His eyes darkened and his hand tightened its grip on her chin.

Then his head lowered and his lips touched hers in a kiss so gentle, so tentative, she might have imagined it.

He pulled away, creating coolness where there was once warmth, distance where there was once closeness.

She murmured a slight protest, leaning toward him again.

"Beth, I need to—"

"Don't talk," she said, slipping her hand around his neck. "Words just get in the way."

Though her practical nature warned her, the part that yearned for the closeness and comfort he offered pulled his head back toward her.

And they kissed again.

Finally Nick drew back, still holding her and Kyle as he leaned back against the couch.

Beth nestled closer to him and as he held her she felt a sense of homecoming she had never felt in Jim's arms.

Jim.

Like a cold breeze, memories of him sifted into the moment. Yet she didn't move away from Nick, promising herself that for just this little while, she would let him hold her up. Let herself be a bit vulnerable.

They sat quietly like this for a while longer, not saying anything, seemingly content to simply be.

Nick stroked her hair away from her face and then he released a heavy sigh. "You know, when I was in Afghanistan, there were times I felt like there was no beauty in the world anymore." He was quiet a moment and he gave a gentle laugh. "That's when I would think about you."

Beth pulled back to look at him, puzzled. "What do you mean?"

Nick traced the contours of her face, his eyes following the path of his finger. "Jim always had a picture of you pinned to the tent wall, like the other guys did with their wives or girlfriends. I would look at the picture and think about you and Jim and your baby. What kind of life you two were going to have when he came back. I would get him to talk about it. To tell me. Sounds kind of weird, but it kept me going. In the middle of the dust and the heat and the tediousness of vehicle repairs, and the tension of driving down long, treacherous roads, I'd hang on to thoughts of your life."

"Really?" Beth frowned, feeling like a bit of a fraud. "Jim had a picture up of me?" she asked, unable to keep the irony out of her voice.

Nick nodded, twining a strand of her hair around his finger. "I felt guilty because I was jealous of him. Jealous that he had someone waiting for him at home. That he had you waiting." Nick looked down at Kyle. "And your baby." A look of sadness crossed his face again.

Beth tried to fit her memories of Jim with the picture Nick created.

"He talked a lot about you." Nick gave her a melancholy smile. "And now I'm here. And not Jim."

Beth touched his cheek as if to reassure him. "It's okay, you know. That you're here."

Nick held her gaze as a gentle smile curved his

lips. "That's good, then." He brushed a kiss over her forehead, then looked down at Kyle, one finger touching his cheek.

"Do you want to hold him?" Beth asked.

Nick hesitated just a moment. "Sure. I guess I could."

Beth frowned at his hesitating. He'd held Kyle before. What was the problem?

She gently slipped Kyle into his arms and as her baby settled, she sat back, smiling at the picture of her tiny, fragile baby in the arms of this large, burly soldier.

Nick jostled Kyle a bit, as if he felt he should do something with this bundle. Then he sat back, pulling his knees up to cradle him. He looked down at Kyle and the tenderness in his face created a sliver of hope in Beth. She couldn't imagine Jim doing this, no matter what Nick said about him. No matter what visions Nick had of their relationship. She knew, without a doubt, that Jim would never have been the father that she saw glimpses of in Nick.

"You look natural doing that."

A light frown creased his forehead. "Well, I don't feel real natural. He feels small and helpless."

"He is," Beth agreed, leaning forward to look at Kyle in Nick's arms. "These little ones are so defenseless, aren't they?" She ran her finger over Kyle's tender cheek.

"Not helping things," Nick said with a nervous laugh.

Beth had to smile at his discomfort. Moments ago he had been a man in charge, now he looked as if he wasn't sure how to hold this baby.

"You're doing okay," she said quietly.

Nick released a light sigh as he shifted Kyle in his arms. His eyes flickered over Kyle's face, his mouth curving up in a pensive smile.

"Who does he look like?" Nick asked.

"I don't know. I'm not good at this kind of thing. I think he looks like Kyle."

Nick tipped his head to one side, then the other, his gaze flicking from Kyle to Beth.

"He seems to favor you more than Jim. Jim had a bigger nose and Kyle seems to have your heart-shaped face."

"I hope the poor child doesn't get my hair."

"What's wrong with your hair?" Nick frowned, as if he couldn't understand what she was talking about.

Beth self-consciously tucked her hair back behind her ears. "It gets all out of control and in damp weather it goes every which way."

"You don't wear it down much, do you?"

"No. Jim used to say I looked like a walking scouring pad when I did."

"Why would he say that?"

Beth shrugged. Why would Jim say many of the things he said? "Because it was true?"

"I think you need a second opinion," Nick said, letting Kyle rest in the cradle his legs created. He reached over and before Beth could protest, he pulled her hair forward, fluffing it around her face.

"I hate to say this about my buddy, but Jim was wrong." Nick's gentle smile slipped behind her already crumbling defenses. "You look beautiful."

His compliment nourished her hungry soul. She held his sincere gaze and for a heartbeat she allowed herself to wonder.

To dream.

"Have you had a serious girlfriend?" Beth asked, trying to bring herself back to reality.

Nick didn't say anything right away and Beth wished she could take the question back.

"Once upon a time I did," he said finally. "But she broke up with me before my first tour. Said she couldn't take the stress."

"I'm sorry. I didn't mean—"

"It's okay. I knew she wasn't right for me. We

sort of stayed together because neither of us felt right in breaking up the relationship. So she took the first move and it was for the best. At least that's what Jim always told me," Nick added with a smile as if to show her that it truly didn't matter to him.

Beth tore her gaze away from his and looked down at Kyle, still sleeping peacefully on Nick's lap. She stroked her son's cheek, her emotions a confused tangle.

"Did Jim really talk that much about me?"

Nick looked down at Kyle and tucked the tip of his forefinger into Kyle's tiny hand. "He had to. I was always asking questions about you."

Bewilderment clouded her mind. Who had Jim really been? The man Nick knew for six months, or the man she had known for six years?

Beth wanted to believe Nick but Jim's words had never meant much before. For all she knew what Jim had told Nick were just empty words, too, meant to fill the tediousness and tension of the long drives.

Kyle stirred, releasing a sigh that slowly changed into a squawk. He squirmed in Nick's arms, his squawk turning into a cry. Beth took Kyle from Nick, only too glad to focus on something present. On Kyle.

"I should go," she murmured.

Without looking at Nick, she got up and walked up the stairs to her room, holding Kyle close to her, his protests growing with each step.

She closed the door and sat down to feed Kyle. As she held her baby close, her thoughts became a tangle of attraction, happiness and perplexity. What was she doing? She was a recently widowed woman. Sure, her plans to move away and set up her own place had been put on hold, but only temporarily.

Beth looked down at Kyle, quiet now, his downy head lying against her, his tiny fist curling and uncurling as he drank. So precious.

Completely dependent on her and completely dependent on the decisions she would make. Whatever she decided in her life would have an effect on him.

At the same time her thoughts drifted downstairs to the man waiting below.

Beth touched her lips with her fingertips as if seeking evidence of Nick's kiss. Was this right? Was she allowed to have this dream of her and Nick?

Did she dare?

What had he done?

Nick clasped his hands over his neck, bending

his head. *Lord, forgive me,* he prayed. *This can't be right.*

Another thought entered his mind. *You didn't do this alone. Beth was a willing participant. But she is grieving and alone, and I took advantage of that.*

Nick strode to the window and stood, looking out into the darkness, his hands planted on his hips.

Things were easier back in the field. You followed orders, you did what you were told. You grieved the loss of some men and you moved on. You stayed tough, stoic, because that's what soldiers do.

But this?

He was out here without a map. Without directions or orders. The plan he had in place when he came here was blown away when Bob hurt himself.

When he saw Beth face-to-face.

He shoved his hand through his hair and blew out a sigh. He felt as if he had crossed the wire, a boundary he had put in place to survive. Beth was out of bounds for him. She was Jim's wife and he had no right to have feelings for her.

He should get back to the other house and keep

his distance from her. And he would. But first he had to say goodbye to Beth.

Half an hour later, she still hadn't come downstairs, and full of concern, Nick went upstairs. She lay on her bed with Kyle curled up against her. Both of them were fast asleep.

Nick looked down at the sight, his heart full. She was probably exhausted after crying so hard and long. He knelt beside the bed and gently stroked her cheek. Then he laid his hand on Kyle's tiny body, his heart full.

Could this be happening? Could there be a future for them?

Chapter Ten

"The doctor figures it will be at least four weeks before I'm fully mobile," Bob said with a note of disgust in his voice. It was Monday evening and Ellen had come home only a couple of hours previously with a querulous Bob in tow.

Bob forked a piece of steak into his mouth and chewed vigorously, as if taking his frustration with his doctor out on the meat. He shot a look at Nick over the kitchen table. "You don't have to figure on sticking around that long. I'm not some charity case."

"I'll stay as long as I need to," Nick assured Bob.

"That's asking too much of you," Bob protested.

Nick shrugged. "I don't have anywhere else to go and no one else waiting for me."

Beth knew Nick wasn't looking for sympathy, but the casual way he tossed the words out disturbed her.

Though her brother Art had been relieved she wouldn't be moving in with him after all, he still told her if she really, desperately needed a place, she was probably welcome to stay. Beth had ignored all the conditions that came with his offer and accepted it for what it was. And her mother, bless her heart, had offered to come and stay if Beth really needed her to.

They were flawed but they were still family.

Nick had no one.

At that moment his gaze captured hers and she hoped her sympathy didn't show on her face. She knew he wouldn't appreciate it.

But he gave her a quick smile that transformed his features and shifted her heart. She felt a sense of rightness and a connection with Nick that she had never felt with Jim. She couldn't look away, nor did she want to as images from last night drifted into her mind. Memories of his arms around her, supporting her as her sorrow overcame her.

"What do you think, Beth?"

With a start, Beth realized Ellen had been talking to her. A flush warmed her cheeks as she looked over at her mother-in-law. "I'm sorry, Ellen. What were you saying?"

Ellen glanced from her to Nick who was concentrating on the food on his plate, trying to look nonchalant.

"The church is having a dessert evening and auction to help raise money for some of the youth who will be going to Haiti to help out there." Ellen gave Beth a tight smile which made Beth guess that she had seen the exchange between her and Nick.

"That's nice," Beth murmured, wondering why Ellen was telling her this.

"I told the lady organizing it that maybe you could donate some of your cards."

Beth thought of the cards she had already made, gathering dust in her craft room. "I don't know," she said with a quick shrug. "I don't think they would sell."

"Why not? They're so unique and anything handmade is so much more meaningful than what you can buy in the store. Unless you don't want to donate them, of course," Ellen added hastily.

"No. No. I don't mind donating them. They're not doing anything sitting in my office right now."

"Do you really think they would sell, Ellen?" Bob asked, looking up from his food. "People buy jam and pies and quilts and sweaters at the church fundraisers," Bob continued. "You know, stuff you can use." He gave Beth a quick smile. "No offense, honey. I like your cards and they're real pretty, but what do you do with them?"

Beth knew her father-in-law meant no harm, but his easy dismissal of what she loved doing hurt just a bit.

"I would buy some," Ellen snapped.

"You wouldn't need to," Beth said quietly. "I've got so many I would gladly give them—"

Ellen shot her a stern glance. "I would buy a dozen."

Beth wondered why her mother-in-law seemed so upset. Had she guessed what had happened between Nick and Beth while she was gone? Should they have gone to church yesterday?

All day Beth felt as if Ellen was watching her, looking for some evidence of behavior between Nick and Beth she could only speculate about. She wanted to tell Ellen that nothing had happened, but Beth knew she would be lying.

Something had happened—some major and elemental shift in Beth's life that she didn't dare look too closely at. She wasn't sure what to think or what to allow herself to think.

She had to keep her priorities straight.

But yet…

"What about you, Nick? What do you think about Beth's cards?"

Beth squirmed, wishing Ellen hadn't put Nick on the spot like that. Someone who had been through what Nick had wouldn't put much value on pieces of paper cut up and glued together to make something as fleeting as a card to express a sentiment.

Nick pulled in one corner of his mouth, as if considering the question. "I think that everyone needs a bit of pretty in their lives. Something to cheer them up."

"Why do you say that?" Bob shot Nick a puzzled look. "I didn't think you were the touchy-feely type."

Beth felt a tiny jolt, as well. She couldn't imagine why Nick defended a hobby even Jim had sneered at.

Nick sat back in his chair, his arms folded over his chest. "When we were stationed in Kandahar, one of the guys had written home and gotten his parents to send him some grass seed. He built a raised bed out of old lumber in front of his tent, no bigger than a foot and a half by five feet and maybe four inches high. He scrounged enough dirt to fill the bed. He planted the grass and somehow got enough water in that desert climate to water it." Nick eased out a wry smile. "It grew. It was this tiny patch of green in the middle of an ocean of heat, dust and brown camo. It served no purpose, but it raised morale." Nick's gaze ticked over Bob then Ellen and came to rest on Beth. "We used to run our hands over it, to remind us of home. Some guys would step carefully on it before they went out on a mission. For luck, I guess. But we needed that patch of grass to remind us that there is beauty in the world."

Beth couldn't look away as Nick spoke, surprised at the undercurrent of emotion in his voice and touched by his story.

"I think what Beth does isn't a whole lot different," Nick continued.

"I don't think my cards can rate quite the same as that hopeful patch of grass in Afghanistan," she said quietly.

"I think they can," Nick said. "I think they're important in their own way. I think they can bring beauty into someone's life. And a smile."

Beth's face flushed again at his gentle defense of her.

"I agree with Nick." Ellen spoke up. "And I

know you've got a bunch of them ready to go, Beth, so it would be real nice if you could take some along."

"I don't know," Beth murmured, still not convinced. In spite of Ellen's declaration, Beth wasn't sure she wanted to donate cards she had put so much effort and care into only to suffer the humiliation of not having them sell.

"I do know," Ellen announced, her voice brooking no argument. "After the dishes we're going over to the other house and picking out some cards. And I'm buying tickets for you and Nick so that you can come with us. And you'll see how they do for yourself."

And that, apparently, was that.

"How is my grandson?" Bob asked, thankfully shifting the conversation to more comfortable territory. "He sleep good last night?"

With relief, Beth latched on to her favorite subject.

They talked about Kyle, about how much he was growing and how cute he was. From there they moved to the cows, the weather and events going on in the community.

When supper was over, Nick said he and Bob would clean up, leaving Ellen and Beth free to go.

Kyle still slept so Beth couldn't use him as an excuse to not pick out cards. Ten minutes later she and Ellen were walking side by side through the dark cold.

Beth slipped her hands in the pockets of her jacket, struggling not to feel suddenly self-conscious. She felt as if every kiss Nick had given her was branded on her lips for Ellen and Bob to see.

"I'm glad that Kyle is doing well," Ellen said as they approached the house. "He seems to be sleeping better."

Beth only nodded.

"I hope you're not too nervous taking care of him after what happened last night."

"I am. A bit," Beth confessed as she opened the door of the house and flicked on the light. "When I took him in to the medi-center this morning the doctor there said his chest was clear and he was in no danger. Which is a blessing. I thought maybe he would be a bit more congested but the doctor didn't seem to think Kyle was, so I guess I shouldn't worry so much." Beth pressed her lips together, putting a brake on her babbling.

Beth sensed the trip to get the cards was a ruse

so Ellen could talk to her about what she suspected happened last night. Beth just wanted to get the "talk" over and done with.

But Ellen said nothing as she glanced around the main floor. "Nick is a very tidy person," she said approvingly.

"He's a soldier. Jim was the same way," Beth said, pleased herself to see the house looking neater than when she left it.

"I suppose he was."

Was she imagining the terse note in Ellen's voice, Beth wondered as she walked carefully up the narrow stairs.

"I know we drilled neatness into him," Ellen continued, her voice quiet. "But as a parent, you can only teach your children so much."

Beth didn't know what to say to that vague comment, so she wisely kept her words to herself.

Beth opened the door of her craft room and felt a tiny pulse of expectation when she saw the table, paper piled up on one side, ribbon lying in a tangle on the other. Rows of jars filled with colorful flowers, brads and buttons for embellishing the cards stood lined up against the wall. Her cutting machine was still open and the cutting mat lay beside it uncovered. Beth closed it, picked up a spool of ribbon and rolled it up, trying not to fuss.

Jim often chided her about working in a mess, wondering how she could do it. But this was how she worked best. She needed to have everything available and she needed the stimulation of the colors and fibers surrounding her.

Her finished cards, however, were set out in neat rows on a shelf above her desk.

"You usually put some kind of poem inside, don't you?" Ellen asked.

"Only if I'm giving it to someone specific."

Beth wondered if Ellen and Bob knew that she'd made up the poems she put in the cards she gave them. There were so many things she wanted to tell them, but doing it with a poem in a card was easier than speaking the words aloud.

"So these are all ready to go?" Ellen asked, plucking a bright red card decorated with a paper owl off the shelf.

Beth nodded, trying to see the cards she had put so much of herself into through her practical mother-in-law's eyes. They did seem frivolous and pointless. A waste of time and paper and resources, Jim always said.

Yet Beth's gaze flitted over the table, her hands itching to start cutting and pasting. She picked up a tube of peach embossing powder that she had bought just before Kyle was born. She turned it back and forth, letting the light of the room play over the glistening powder. It would look lovely on a sage-green card and she had the perfect stamp to use with it.

"I like this one." Ellen pulled a purple card down, as well.

"This one is beautiful, too. Oh, and this one is cute."

Ellen worked her way along the shelf, commenting on each of the cards, picking some, leaving some behind. Beth let Ellen do the choosing, assuming she would know better which ones would go over well in the community.

She still thought the whole enterprise was a waste of time, but to her surprise Ellen seemed determined. After about twenty minutes, Ellen had narrowed her selection down to fifteen cards. "We don't want to donate too many," she explained when she put some of her initial choices back. "If there's too many, it decreases the value of them."

"I don't think there's a huge value anyway." Beth fingered the satin ribbon she had just rolled back up on a spool.

"More than you might think," Ellen insisted. "Now, do you have anything we can put these cards in to protect them?"

Beth pulled open a drawer of her desk and pulled out a number of glassine bags. "I bought these to use."

Ellen held out one card, frowning at it.

"What's wrong?" Beth asked.

Ellen pursed her lips, then shook her head. "I'm surprised that you haven't held a workshop at Shellie's store to show people how to make them."

"Shellie told me she didn't think anyone would be interested in a craft class."

"Then why didn't she try to sell them for you? In the store. They are so unique. I'm sure people would buy them."

Beth shrugged aside her suggestion. "Shellie didn't think they would sell."

Ellen gave a curt nod. "Well, we'll see about that."

Beth didn't bother to ask her what she meant. Her mind was still preoccupied with thoughts of last night. She still felt bad that she had fallen asleep before she'd had a chance to thank Nick again.

She'd woken up in the middle of the night and

realized what had happened. Then she couldn't fall asleep anymore. All she could think about was Nick holding her. Nick kissing her.

She wondered what it meant and where their relationship would go and what she would do about it. When she had finally fallen asleep again, her dreams were a tangled montage of Nick, Kyle and Jim.

"So I'll phone Louisa—she's the organizer—and tell her I've got another donation."

They put the cards in the bags and then Beth glanced at her watch. Kyle had been sleeping for over two hours now.

"I'm sure the boys will call us if Kyle wakes up," Ellen assured her, understanding Beth's concern.

Beth nodded, waiting for her mother-in-law to head out the door, but she stood in front of Beth, shuffling the cards in her hands.

"I…uh…am guessing that you and Nick spent some time together yesterday," Ellen said quietly.

Beth's mind fumbled for the best words to use as a flood of guilt flushed her cheeks. "After Nick helped me with Kyle…he stayed awhile. Just to make sure Kyle was okay."

She stopped herself before she released words Ellen couldn't sympathize with or understand. Beth could not tell Jim's mother that only a few months after Jim's death, she'd kissed another man—and enjoyed it.

Ellen traced a raised image that Beth had embossed on one of the cards, her mouth curved up in a wry smile. "I think Nick is a good man," she said quietly. "He's done a lot for us."

What was Ellen trying to say?

Was she really trying to encourage Beth to consider Nick?

Chapter Eleven

"What do we do now?" Nick asked, hovering in the doorway of the noisy church hall.

Round tables draped with white tablecloths filled the hall. Each one held coffee cups set on bright red napkins and in the center of the table sat a grouping of candles flickering in red-tinted vases. Tiny lights twinkled from bare trees set strategically around the auditorium, creating a winter-wonderland feel.

The church fundraiser looked festive and welcoming, but no one sat at the tables. Instead they gathered in groups, talking, laughing, looking at auction items displayed on long, covered tables against the walls of the large room. The noise of conversation was a steady buzz. Everyone seemed to know each other.

Ellen and Bob had been sidetracked by some

people in the cloakroom and had told Nick and Beth to go ahead.

So they had and now stood in the hallway, uncertain where to go or what to do.

"I've never been to one of these before," Beth said, glancing around. "Haven't even been to church much."

She stopped going when she found out about Jim's cheating. She hadn't had much to do with church since, as she often worked on Sundays, much to Ellen and Bob's dismay.

Nick touched her on the arm. "By the way, I was wondering if we could—"

"Oh, my goodness, if it isn't Beth Carruthers looking as skinny as all get-out. How are you doing, my dear girl?" A stout woman, her hair a riot of bright red curls, grabbed Beth's arm and pulled her close, interrupting Nick's question. Beth quelled a moment of annoyance at the interruption, caught her balance, then looked down at Jolene Wilkins, a regular at the coffee shop Beth had worked at before her boss pleaded with her to quit. Jolene put her hand on Beth's arm and shook her head in sympathy. "I've been praying for you, my dear. And would you let me see that precious baby? He was early, wasn't he?" Jolene said, gently pulling back the blanket Beth had wrapped around

Kyle. Kyle lay in Beth's arms, fast asleep, one tiny hand curled up beside his cheek, his eyelashes a delicate fan against his pale skin. He stirred, then settled back into his usual deep, peaceful slumber, his tiny lips pursed. "I'm surprised he's out of the hospital already."

"He only had to stay a few days," Beth replied. "He was a good size when he was born so they didn't need to keep him long." Beth shot a glance at Nick who gave her a quick wink. Whatever he wanted to say would have to wait.

"He is so gorgeous. Doesn't look anything like Jim, though." Jolene stroked Kyle's cheek with one pudgy finger. She glanced over at Nick and Beth easily read the puzzlement on Jolene's face.

"Jolene, this is Nick Colter," Beth said, introducing him. "He served with Jim in Afghanistan. He's staying with Bob and Ellen, helping out on the ranch while Bob recuperates." Beth was pleased with how smoothly that came out. She didn't even flush when she said Nick's name.

Jolene's mouth formed a perfect O and she pressed her hand to her ample bosom. "Oh, my goodness. You served with Jim? That was such a tragedy. So sad that he was the only person killed on that mission. He was so young and…well…" She lifted her arms as if to hug him but when Beth saw the horrified look on Nick's face, she came to his rescue.

"We should see what's taking Bob and Ellen so long," Beth said, grasping Nick's arm and pulling him out of Jolene's reach. She gave Jolene an apologetic smile. "I'm a bit worried about Bob since his accident."

"As if Ellen hasn't had enough to deal with," Jolene clucked as she backed away. "Tell Ellen that I just adore the cards she donated. They are going to be a hot-ticket item."

Beth frowned at her enthusiasm, wondering if Ellen had told her to say something. She didn't have a chance to ask Jolene more because Nick pulled her along, beating a hasty retreat.

However, they didn't get far. People were entering the hall and they were stopped a number of times by friends of Bob and Ellen, old acquaintances of Jim and church members. Beth received condolences for Jim and congratulations for Kyle and a few brief hugs. She had never come to church here, yet people knew her name and her circumstances.

By the time Ellen and Bob caught up to them, Beth felt overwhelmed by the outpouring of support she had received from people who barely knew her.

But Nick didn't repeat what he was going to ask her. Much to her dismay.

"You two aren't sitting down yet?" Ellen asked, then led them to a table toward the back. As Beth settled into her chair, more people came by their table to see how Bob was doing, to express their sympathy to Beth and to ooh and aah over Kyle.

And all of them shot curious glances at Nick as if trying to figure out where he fit in the picture.

Nick didn't seem fazed by the attention and Beth was surprised at his aplomb. Grace under fire, she thought.

"This is a warm, welcoming community," Nick said as people slowly found their places at other tables.

Ellen nodded, shooting a glance toward Beth. "People care. I've had lots of friends asking me about Beth and telling me that they are praying for her."

To her surprise, Nick held Beth's gaze across the table. "I'm sure that's why she's been able to be so strong these past few weeks," he said quietly.

How could he say that after she completely dissolved in his arms just the other night? She shot him a puzzled glance, but he just gave her a slow smile.

"Oh, my. So this is the miracle baby."

Beth looked up at Shellie's mother, a tall, slender woman with perfectly coiffed ash-blond hair.

"Hello, Mrs. Cruikshank," Beth said quietly. "How are you doing?"

"Fine. Just fine." Her cool gaze ticked around the table as she adjusted the silk scarf wrapped around her neck. "Congratulations. How is your baby doing now that he's home?" she asked Beth.

Beth looked down at Kyle, warm and snug in her arms. "Very well. He's given us a few scares but overall his health is good."

"A blessing indeed. Shellie told me you were working right until the day he was born." Mrs. Cruikshank gave Beth a tight smile. "Good thing your baby wasn't born in the store."

Beth frowned up at Shellie's mother, not sure if Mrs. Cruikshank was making a joke or a judgment.

"Beth is very responsible," Nick said, coming to her defense. "She wasn't to know that her baby would come so soon."

Mrs. Cruikshank flapped her hands at Nick, as if dismissing her own comments. "Of course she wouldn't." She gave Ellen and Bob a nod. "Congratulations and have a good evening." Then she swept away, leaving Beth feeling as if she had to catch her breath.

"She doesn't seem very friendly, does she?" Nick frowned at Mrs. Cruikshank as she sat down at the far end of the hall.

Beth shrugged again, looking down at her son still sleeping peacefully. "She's okay," Beth said, preferring not to talk about her boss's mother. Mrs. Cruikshank had always been a puzzle to her and Beth had given up trying to understand her veiled antagonism. Beth put up with it because she loved working at Crafty Corners so much.

"Welcome to this evening," a young man said into the microphone at the front of the room, catching their attention. "Nice to see such a large group out. I'm sure a lot of it has to do with the desserts that the Ladies' Auxiliary have promised we'd be getting during the break, but I'm also sure much it is because of the amazing items we're bidding on in a short while. But before we start I'd like to open this evening with a word of prayer."

Beth should have known that anything to do with church usually started with prayer, but it still caught her off guard. However she lowered her head but kept her eyes on Kyle as the young man began to pray. Other than her panicked prayer when Kyle was choking, she hadn't talked much to God lately.

"Dear Lord, we thank You for this opportunity

to be together. Thank You for our community and for the young people that are going to help those less fortunate than us. Help us to support them not only with our money, but with our prayers. Be with us this evening and keep our hearts and wallets open. Amen."

A group of young people made their way to the front of the hall. They introduced a song they were going to sing and with a crash of drums and a burst of guitar chords they began.

Beth caught herself tapping her toe to the music, a song about standing before the throne of grace. The words tweaked a memory and she caught herself humming along.

With the music came another, older, deeper memory.

Standing beside her father in church, his deep bass resonating as he sang with conviction the songs of faith.

Beth remembered looking up to him, her heart full of pride that her father didn't need to look at the words of the song. He taught her Bible verses, taught her hymns, taught her how to tie her shoelaces, ride a bike.

And when he left, promising her he'd come back someday, then never called or wrote or came back, he taught her that words meant nothing.

Beth pressed her lips against the memory, as she kept her eyes firmly fixed on her own child. What would she teach Kyle? What example would she be to him?

What would she tell him about his father?

Life was such a tangle, she thought, swallowing a sudden rush of sorrow and guilt. Then, to her surprise, she felt Nick's hand give her arm a gentle squeeze. She chanced a glance at him and caught his quizzical look followed by a gentle smile.

Nick is a good man.

Her mother-in-law's words slipped into her mind, at once reassuring and puzzling.

It was as if Ellen had given Beth some type of tacit approval because Beth was sure Ellen had an idea of what happened that evening she and Nick were alone.

Could Beth trust her heart to another man when she had been hurt so badly in the past?

She didn't know and for a moment, as the words of the song wrapped themselves around her uncertain heart, she wished that she could pray about this. That she could put her life in God's hands as she had so trustingly done in the past.

"…my name is carved deep in His palm," the singers sang, their voices earnest, sincere. "He knew me when I was unformed, He comes to me with words of love, and whispers that I am His own."

Beth looked away from Nick as the words sifted into her soul. An old longing returned to her and an older love called to her.

Once she'd believed that God would take care of her, but her life had taken twists and turns she hadn't seen coming. Her father had left her, trailing empty promises to return behind. Jim's promises had proved to be as untrustworthy, his words as false.

Yet because of Jim she had Kyle.

She looked down at her sleeping baby and held his warmth just a little closer. This precious child had done nothing, yet his very act of being had created a wellspring of love that was surprising in its intensity.

Did God know Kyle when he was unformed, as the song said? Did God know what a gift this innocent child would be?

She bowed her head and sent up a tiny prayer, thanking God for Kyle. For the gift she didn't deserve, but a gift that she accepted with love and gratitude.

"Is everything okay?" Nick leaned closer to her, whispering to her.

She waited before looking up at him. She caught his earnest gaze, the concern in his eyes.

"Yeah. I think so," she said.

His smile entered her heart and made a home there.

And Nick? Was he a gift, as well?

She didn't know if she dared think that.

Nick shifted his weight in his seat, feeling a twinge of pain from his old injury. He wanted to get up, but he didn't dare in case he missed Beth's cards.

Thankfully, it looked as if they were up next.

"Here we've got a set of cards donated by…" the auctioneer glanced down at a piece of paper and shrugged. "Okay, it says they're donated by Ellen Carruthers but made by Beth Carruthers, so you'll have to figure that one out." The auctioneer held up four cards. "We've got four batches of four cards. Send them to your girlfriend. Send them to your mother. Send them to your pastor if you ain't got one or the other." Polite laughter followed this joke. "Let's open the bidding for the first set. Do I hear twenty? Twenty anywhere? Fifteen? Ten? Five? Oh, c'mon, give me something to work with here. It's for a good cause."

Nick didn't have to look at Beth to feel her

tension. It had to be difficult to see her work put up for such a public display and to have their worth decided by people who didn't know what she had put into them. He waited a moment and then put up his hand, indicating that he bid five dollars.

"Fantastic. Thanks for getting things started here, sir," the auctioneer said. "Do I hear six? Six anywhere?"

Nick knew Beth would think this was a pity gesture on his part and maybe it was. But he couldn't let the price go down any lower. He dared a glance toward Beth, but she was looking down at Kyle, her lips pressed together.

He felt a beat of dismay. Just before they came into the hall he had hoped to ask her out. What she had written in the card she had given him this morning had been vague, but encouraging.

Thanks for your help, your support, your strength. You saved Kyle's life and you redeemed mine. Thanks for letting me lean on you. For now.

He had wanted to capitalize on that when that well-meaning but chatty Jolene woman had interrupted them and the moment was lost in the deluge of sympathy that followed.

After that all he heard people talk about was

Jim, Jim and more Jim. It was like rubbing salt into his already wounded soul and a reminder that Jim was supposed to be here. Not him.

Kyle started fussing and Beth leaped to her feet, gratitude wreathing her features. "I'll go take care of him," she said, then ducked her head and left the room.

"Eight, now nine, now ten. Twelve, now fifteen."

Nick's attention was yanked back to the auctioneer. The price was moving up. He put in another bid at twenty, was outbid, then put in another bid of twenty-five and was outbid again. Twice.

The final bid was sixty-five dollars. The second set sold for seventy. The third for fifty. Beth hadn't returned yet and Nick was disappointed she couldn't have seen for herself what her cards went for.

The final set went up and Nick managed to get the fourth set for eighty-five dollars. Way too much for some bits of paper stuck together, as Bob would say, but it was the designer he was more interested in than the product.

"Well, Beth Carruthers. If you don't have a job already, you should think about starting a card-making business," the auctioneer said as he handed Nick his purchase.

Nick took the cards, gave the woman taking care of the accounting books his name and as he returned to his seat, he saw Beth standing at the back of the room, rocking Kyle.

Her eyes were wide, her cheeks flushed and by the way her mouth hung open Nick suspected she hadn't figured on this outcome. Nick gave her a discreet thumbs-up, thankful that she'd been able to witness this affirmation of what she did.

"That went very well." Ellen's voice held a tinge of pride as Nick set the cards on the table. "And you got my favorite ones."

"I thought I'd have to bid even higher." Nick made a quick decision as he pushed his chair under the table. "I'm going to see how Beth's doing."

Bob frowned, but Ellen gave Nick a quick nod. "That's a good idea," she said with an encouraging smile.

Nick headed to the back of the room but Beth was gone. He glanced around the gathering, but he couldn't see her anywhere.

He was about to go back to the table when he felt a light tap on his shoulder. He turned around to face a younger woman, tall, with reddish hair, flushed cheeks and bright eyes. He frowned, feeling as if he'd seen her before.

"I heard you served with Jim in Afghanistan," she said, shooting nervous glances around the room while she did.

"We were pretty good buddies," he said, wondering what this girl wanted from him.

"I need to talk to you about Jim. Please. In private." She lowered her voice as she took a step closer and slipped a note into his hand. "Please call me and we can arrange to meet." Then, without looking back, she made her way through the hall and left through a side door.

The piece of paper held a phone number. Nothing more. Was this some kind of come-on?

He was tempted to throw it away, but the way the woman asked him made him change his mind. He slipped the note in the pocket of his leather jacket. He'd call her later. Try to figure out what she wanted.

He walked toward the back of the building, where he'd last seen Beth, then saw her in the hallway talking to a young couple.

The smile on her face tugged at his heart. She looked happier than she had in a while.

"…he sleeps really good during the day, but not at night," he heard Beth say.

"Just hang in there, Beth. It will get better," the woman replied.

"I'm sure it will." Beth looked down at Kyle, a loving smile curving her soft lips as she stroked his cheek with her finger.

Her expression created a catch in Nick's throat. He wanted to capture the look on her face and hold on to it.

The woman leaned in a little closer. "He's so adorable." Then the woman caught the hand of a little girl as she came roaring past, her hair streaming behind her. "Slow down, missy. We're going home."

"I'll go start the van," the man said, lifting up a young boy who was yawning and rubbing his eyes.

The woman looked up at Nick, then grinned. "And here's the guy who scooped me on that last batch of cards."

Nick gave a good-natured shrug, his eyes still on Beth. "Highest bidder wins."

"Maybe. Maybe not." The woman turned back to Beth. "Just let me know when you get them ready and I'll come by and pick them up."

Nick gave Beth a puzzled look.

"Trina just asked me to make her a dozen cards," Beth said, her smile warming Nick's heart.

"I wish you could come on board with me," Trina said with a shake of her head. "You've got some great ideas. I really think we could compete with Shellie, though I heard some rumors that her store might be coming up for sale."

"Compete?" Nick asked, puzzled at the reference.

"Trina runs a home-based business, selling scrapbook and card supplies on the internet," Beth explained.

"Really? Card supplies?" He couldn't imagine there would be much money in that.

"It's a billion-dollar industry," Trina returned, a hint of frustration in her voice, as if she'd read his mind.

"Don't get her started," Trina's husband said with a good-natured laugh.

"Think about what I told you," Trina said to Beth. She turned to Nick. "If you ever want to sell those cards, call me."

"I doubt I will," he said.

Trina hesitated a moment, then gave him a careful smile. "I heard you served with Jim."

Nick nodded.

Trina gave him a sympathetic smile. Nick sensed what was coming and mentally braced himself. "I heard that you and Jim were on the same tour when he died. It was certainly tragic that he was the only one who died," she added, her eyes flicking to Beth.

Nick's smile tightened. What could he say? It was tragic. Unfair and many other things that kept him sleeping fitfully at night.

Trina cleared her throat then turned back to Beth. "I'll be praying for you. And Kyle," she said.

Her daughter tugged on her arm. "Mommy, let's go," she complained.

"Sorry. I gotta get going," Trina said, then with a wave she was gone.

Nick watched her go, his own feelings a tumbled stew of sorrow, regret and guilt.

It *was* tragic that Jim was the only one who had died. Tragic, and completely his fault.

Chapter Twelve

"I'd like to get the calf shelters fixed up," Bob said, leaning on his crutches as he and Nick stood in the corrals. "A couple of them have been rotting away and I've never had a chance to repair them."

Nick nodded, unzipping his coat as he leaned against the sun-warmed wood of the corral fence. The sun was gaining strength and warmth.

Bob shifted his weight on his crutches and squinted up at the sun with a smile. "Spring is comin'," he said with authority. "It's a promise God makes us every winter, and every spring He comes through. This whole creation is His, that's for sure. And He's in charge."

"Of this part at least."

Bob shot him a sideways glance. "What are you saying, son?"

"I guess I saw so much in Afghanistan it was hard to believe God occupied that corner of the world," Nick said, looking out over the snow-covered fields beyond the corrals. He let the utter peace of the place soak in and nourish him. He didn't want to think about what he would do when it was time to go.

For now, he was here. For now, it had to be enough.

"I'm sure you saw your share of pain and suffering," Bob agreed. "Jim never wrote much, so we didn't hear a lot, but we got an idea whenever we'd get hold of him."

Nick's mind flashed back to Jim dying in his arms. He tried to push the picture away because with the memory came the guilt.

"It was hard," Nick agreed. "And it was hard to see God there."

"I guess it's easy for me to say that He was. I don't know what you've had to deal with. I've seen death, but not like you have. I like to believe all those sacrifices were for a reason. And God kept you safe and that's a blessing, isn't it?" Bob said.

Nick couldn't believe what he heard. "But your son died."

"He did. And that's been hard to deal with but thanks to God we're pulling through." Bob eased out a sigh. "But for you, I think it's important to count your own personal blessings. I think it's a way of realizing God is working in your life."

Nick couldn't say anything to that. Lately he missed the presence of God in his life and he knew that turning his back on Him didn't change the fact that God was still there. He couldn't wish God away.

They stood in silence, watching the cows, heads buried in the feeders, eating the hay Nick had just brought out for them. Bob had come just to watch. Needed to get out of the house, he said. Too many women. But Nick sensed that in spite of his gruff talk, he enjoyed having Beth and the baby in the house.

"You ever figure out what you're going to do after you're finished helping out this charity case?" Bob asked.

"You're not a charity case." Nick lifted his own injured leg and hooked the heel of his boot on the bottom rung of the corral fence. "I don't mind helping."

"I sure appreciate the help you've given in the meantime." Bob put his crutches in front of him and leaned on them, squinting out over the fields, his cowboy hat pushed back on his head. "You're a good man."

"Just trying to be live up to my parents' expectations," Nick said.

"They church people?" Bob asked.

Nick had to smile at the term. "Yeah. They were."

"You don't go to church anymore?"

"Not after they died. I was angry with God. And then, when I joined the army, I had other things on my mind."

"And then you did a number of tours in Afghanistan," Bob added.

Nick said nothing.

"You miss church?" Bob asked.

Nick mulled over that question a moment, then sighed. "Yeah. Sometimes I do."

"You should come this Sunday. Won't hurt you. Might help you."

"I'll think about it," Nick said.

"Don't bother thinking," Bob replied. "Just come."

Nick smiled again. "Maybe I will."

Bob and Nick were silent awhile, watching the animals.

"How many quarters you have?" Nick finally asked.

"Too many," Bob said with a sigh.

"Why too many?"

"When I first bought this place I had small plans. Then, after Jim was born, the plans got bigger. I bought more land and leased more land and got more cows." Bob released a heavy sigh. "Now, I've got this spread, something I've put my heart and soul into, and no one to pass it on to."

"You've got Kyle," Nick said.

"I won't be able to keep this place going long enough for him to take it over. And what if he's like his daddy? Hates ranching and anything to do with it?"

Surprise jolted Nick. "Jim hated ranching? That wasn't the impression I got."

Bob shrugged. "Jim's my son, but he always had a tendency to tell a body what a body wanted to hear. Jim was never a rancher. Never had the patience, never had the love of animals and the land." Bob shot him a sideways squint. "Not like I see in you."

Nick tried to understand what Bob said about Jim to what he and Jim had talked so often about. Ranching and cows and breeds and branding and riding out on the range and checking fences and haying, which made Nick homesick for what he'd lost that horrible day his parents died.

It didn't match what Bob said.

Then Bob cleared his throat. "You ever think about going back into ranching, son?"

"It's a dream long past," Nick said.

"Your leg ain't that much of a problem."

"The leg's not the problem." Nick pushed himself away from the fence. "I had to sell my parents' ranch to pay the bills. There's no way I could afford to buy it back now."

"There's other ranches," Bob said. "I hate to see this one get into the hands of some hobby farmer. Someone with more money than love of the land. I'd like to see someone who really cares in charge of this place and I'd be willing to help that person out."

Nick sensed another meaning in Bob's vague words. Was he offering Nick an opportunity to take over this place?

Nick dismissed the thought as unworthy of him. Jim was the one who should be taking over this place.

And it was because of him that Jim wasn't here.

You have to tell him what really happened.

Nick clenched his fists, wishing he could avoid this conversation. But he knew that before he left—and he *was* leaving—that he had to tell Bob the truth about Jim's death. How he and Jim had traded places that day. How, if things had gone the way they were supposed to, Nick would have been in the passenger seat and Nick would have taken the sniper's bullet.

He took a breath, willing the words to come when the whinnying of the horses caught Bob's attention.

Bob fitted his crutches under his arm and stumped toward the fence to investigate and Nick lost the opportunity.

"Looks like Beth's out for a walk again," Bob grunted.

Against his better judgment Nick let his eyes be drawn to the sight of the woman who had been on his mind night and day.

Lately, every time he saw her, his heart gave a traitorous jump and he had to fight the urge to run over, talk to her, connect with her.

Beth walked down the driveway, her arms cradling Kyle under the bulky coat she always wore when she was outside.

She had her head down and she created a forlorn figure, silhouetted against the white snow. He wanted to rush over to her, but his guilt kept him away. Since the fundraiser two days ago, she had kept her distance and he had kept his. As if they both agreed the changing feelings between them were dangerous. Frightening.

"Girl's got a lot on her plate," Bob said quietly. "Lots to have to deal with."

"I'm sure she doesn't need more complications in her life," Nick added, reading the warning in Bob's voice.

As he turned, he caught Bob looking at him, a frown pulling his heavy eyebrows together. Bob opened his mouth as if to speak, but before he could warn Nick off Jim's wife, Nick spoke up.

"So how long do you need to be on those crutches?" he asked.

Bob pursed his lips. "Doc said another week or so. I imagine, once I'm more mobile, you'll want to get out of here."

Nick sent another glance over his shoulder at Beth. Did he really want to leave?

If he was honest with himself, the answer was no.

"Not that I don't like helping you," he said to Bob, "but I should probably be getting on with my life."

Bob frowned but Nick hardened himself to that. This was Bob's place and he was just a sojourner. He couldn't stick around forever, playing at being a rancher, pretending that he and Beth could really build on the foundation of his messy life.

These were dreams out of his reach. He had to face reality and sooner would be better than later. He had to start making plans for the next part of his life.

"Ellen was wondering if you'd come to dinner tonight," Bob asked.

Nick let the idea settle a moment. Dinner with the Carrutherses. And Beth.

He missed her so much it hurt at times. Yet he knew spending more time with her wouldn't be wise. Besides, in spite of their few moments of closeness, he sensed Beth's retreat into the same silence she'd wrapped herself in when he first came. He'd foolishly thought that she'd open up over time, but if anything, she held herself in more tightly.

"I don't know. I don't think so."

"Ellen's been wondering if she did something wrong," Bob continued. "Thinks you don't want to eat her food anymore."

"That's not true. It's just…" Nick let the sentence hang, unable to finish it.

"Then at least stop by for dessert."

"I'll think about it," was all he could say.

"I think Beth misses you, too," Bob added.

Nick's thoughts whirled. He shouldn't think about Beth. He had no right.

"I'll get the lumber for the fence if you get me the nails and hammer," he said to Bob, pushing himself away from the fence.

A few minutes later he was pounding nails into the boards with a fierceness that betrayed his own emotions. He tried to lose himself in the work but as he lifted and pounded, Bob's words resounded in his mind.

"Nick, how wonderful you could join us." Ellen looked up from loading the dishwasher, her smile full of pleasure.

The plate Beth held slipped out of her grasp. She caught it in time but didn't look around.

What was Nick doing here now?

He'd been avoiding her since the fundraiser. She didn't know what had happened there but something had kept him away. His distance had hurt and, as a result, she pulled back into herself, as well. They hadn't talked since that night.

"Bob said I should stop by and say hello."

Just the sound of his voice was enough to send tremors of awareness flickering down her spine. She didn't have to look at him to imagine his face, the way his eyes crinkled when he smiled.

"That's wonderful. We were just going to have

coffee and dessert in the living room." Ellen wiped her hands and walked past Beth to the kettle whistling on the stove.

Beth's hands slowed, trying to make the job last. But eventually she came to the last plate and then there was nothing more to do and no reason not to turn around.

Nick stood by the table, his hands shoved into the back pockets of his blue jeans, his eyes on her. Beth swallowed and tried to look away, but couldn't.

"I made some apple crisp," Ellen said. "With ice cream."

"How can I say no to that?" Nick flashed Ellen a quick smile and looked back at Beth. She wiped her hands down the sides of her pants, then walked over to Kyle who was lying in her father-in-law's arms. Ellen stood behind Bob, smiling at the baby over his shoulder.

"Look how alert he is," she said, amazement tingeing her voice.

"He's been staring at me the past ten minutes," Bob said, a huge grin splitting his face. "I think he knows who I am. I'm pretty sure he smiled at me."

"That's just gas, honey." Ellen patted Bob on the

shoulder. "Shall we go into the living room, or do you want to stay here?"

"Let's go where it's a bit more comfortable." Bob shifted himself to the edge of his chair. Beth was about to take Kyle from him but Ellen beat her to Bob's side.

"Guess I'm never going to have a chance to hold that kid," Nick said with a laugh as Ellen curved her arms around the baby.

"Oh, my goodness, of course you can," Ellen said as she slipped Kyle into Nick's arms, adjusting the blanket around him.

"Hey, little guy," Nick said, his voice soft and gentle. "You're getting to be a real little person with your eyes open." He reached up and stroked Kyle's cheek with his pinky.

The sight of her baby in Nick's arms created an empty ache deep in Beth's soul. She too easily remembered the last time he had done so. Right behind that came the memory of the kisses they'd shared.

She turned away, her cheeks flushing. Why had he been avoiding her? Had he regretted that moment of closeness?

Why had he bought her cards at the fundraiser then acted since then as if she wasn't even alive? Was he just playing with her?

She scurried into the living room, doubts and frustration trailing behind her.

But the only empty seat was on the couch and Nick eased himself into the other cushion beside her.

"I thought we would read from Psalm 127 today," Bob said. "I know I'm skipping around, but these days Ellen and I have simply been looking for words of comfort and hope."

He cleared his throat and began.

"'Unless the Lord builds the house, its builders labor in vain. Unless the Lord watches over the city the watchmen stand in guard in vain...'"

Beth wrapped her arms around herself while Bob read, wishing she had the distraction of her son in her arms. If she was holding Kyle she could focus on him instead of being distracted by Nick sitting only a foot away from her. Nick, who was starting to mean more to her than he should.

And why are you thinking of him while Bob is reading the Bible?

With a guilty start she snapped her attention back to Bob.

"'...sons are a heritage from the Lord, children a reward from him.'"

Bob closed the Bible and set it aside as he cleared his throat, looking directly at Beth. "I know we lost Jim, but Beth, I feel that you and Kyle have been our heritage and reward, as well. I want to say how thankful I am for you and for the past few weeks. I know it hasn't been easy living with the relatives, but it has given us a chance to get to know you better and I'm thankful for that."

"I'd like to add a bit to that," Ellen said. "I knew it would be a blessing to have a grandchild, but having you and Kyle right here in the house with us has been amazing."

Their words created a low-level discomfort in Beth. Though they filled an emptiness in her heart, at the same time they resurrected the guilt that was her constant companion.

How could she tell them she was leaving? How could she take their precious grandchild away from them?

She stole another glance across the couch at her son in Nick's arms. Where did Nick fit into her life? Did she dare let him in?

Nick still looked down at Kyle, unaware of the confusion he created in her.

He looks peaceful, she thought. For the first time since she'd met him, his features held a serene look and she couldn't look away.

As if sensing her regard he looked up at her,

and as their eyes met it was as if their every touch, every shared look was awakened.

Beth felt her breath grow shallow and her heart quicken. This man created feelings and emotions she had never shared with Jim. He frightened her and excited her at the same time. He created a need she knew would be a vulnerability.

She tore her gaze away, unable to look at Ellen and Bob, her face flushed with the guilt she felt was stamped on her every feature.

"I also want to say to you, Nick, what a blessing you've been," Bob continued. "I'm really thankful you were generous enough to stay around and help us out when I needed it."

"Your help meant a lot to both Bob and I," Ellen added. "It was self-sacrificing on your part and to me, shows a real strength of character."

As Nick murmured some noncommittal reply a curious sensation arose in Beth at Bob and Ellen's words.

Was she reading the situation right?

It almost seemed, to her, as if Ellen and Bob were giving them tacit approval to feelings Beth hardly dared acknowledge.

She shook her head to dismiss the thought as one of her overactive imagination. Of the need she felt to give the emotions swirling around her own life a place to grow.

In spite of her guilt over her attraction to Nick, she also knew, on another level, that allowing Nick in her life would change too much. Would move her on a path she didn't dare go down.

Letting Nick into her life would mean opening herself up to pain and the possibility of more betrayal and loss. Her father had left. Jim had left, more than once.

Could she deliberately put herself and Kyle through that?

She looked at Nick again, as if testing her wavering emotions. But his gaze was locked on her son. Kyle's tiny fingers were curled around his thumb.

Beth swallowed an unexpected swell of melancholy. Nick looked right holding Jim's baby.

"I'd like to pray, if we may," Bob said.

Beth eagerly dropped her head. Right about now she needed wisdom and guidance, and if God could give her that, all the better.

What shall I do, Lord? she prayed. *I don't know what to do.*

She pressed her hands to her face, waiting for the revelation.

A peculiar thing happened as Bob prayed.

Instead of a blinding flash of insight, instead of being bathed in wisdom and knowledge, a gentle peace slipped into her soul. A quieting of the voices raging in her mind.

Be still and know that I am God.

The Bible passage eased over the troubled waters of her mind. She clung to it, drawing nourishment into her parched and burdened soul.

She prayed along with Bob. She prayed for Nick. She prayed for herself and, as she prayed, she felt another, deeper prayer slip into her mind.

Lord, I forgive Jim.

As the words resonated in her mind, she felt a burden of anger drop off her shoulders. For the first time since she'd found out about Jim's unfaithfulness, she felt free. She was sure the anger would come back from time to time, but at this moment she felt genuinely free.

For now, it would be enough.

When Bob was finished she kept her head lowered awhile longer, gathering her scattered senses, enjoying this moment of utter peace. Then she raised her head and glanced sideways.

Nick was watching her, as well. She knew she cared for him and her feelings for him were stronger than any she had ever felt for a man.

And forgiving Jim seemed to clear one more

obstacle between her and Nick. She gave him a tentative smile and when he returned it, her heart hitched in response.

The ringing of the phone shattered the moment.

"Who could that be?" Ellen grumbled, grabbing the phone from the receiver beside her chair. "Hello?" she said, getting to her feet. "No, of course not. No, we don't mind coming at all." She shot a glance at Bob, covering the receiver of the phone. "That was Martha. She is very upset, and would like us to come right away." She shot a glance at Nick and Beth. "Would you mind terribly if we left right now?"

Beth shook her head, unsure of what was expected of her. "Of course not."

Ellen walked to the kitchen, still talking on the phone.

Bob slowly got to his feet, and gave Beth and Nick an apologetic smile. "Sorry to duck out on you, but when her old friend Martha calls, Ellen's got to be there."

Ellen returned from the kitchen with her and Bob's coats. "You two don't have to go," Ellen said, giving Bob his coat. "Just stay and visit for a bit."

Beth glanced from Bob to Ellen, trying to understand what they were doing. She didn't want to object, but at the same time their encouragement to spend time together seemed a bit odd.

"We'll be back in about an hour or so," Ellen said. "Please stay until we get back."

Then, a few minutes later, they were gone.

Nick still held Kyle and in the silence following Ellen and Bob's departure, Beth heard her son's snuffling breath.

She swallowed a sudden jolt of awareness. She and Nick were alone and it seemed to her that Ellen and Bob condoned it.

Nick cleared his throat and Beth glanced his way. His gaze held hers and she couldn't look away.

Nick gave her a careful smile.

"What are you thinking?" he asked, reaching across the couch and touching her hand. The feel of his rough fingers on her raised a storm of emotions that had as much to do with how he looked at her as it had to do with his touch.

She wanted to spill the words crowding in her throat. Wanted to tell him how much she had come to care for him. How she trusted him. How she needed him.

"I don't know what to think," she admitted.

Kyle squirmed and Beth used her son as an

excuse to move a little closer. She touched his cheek with one finger.

"He's an amazing gift," Nick said quietly.

"He is," Beth agreed. "I think God knew I needed him at this point in my life even though I was disappointed when I found out that I was pregnant."

"You were disappointed? Why?" The surprise in Nick's voice made her look up at him.

She held his puzzled gaze, wishing she could tell him exactly why. She thought of how often he'd talked about Jim and the illusion he'd created about their marriage. An illusion that, apparently, had carried Nick through some dark days.

Did it matter anymore what he thought of Jim?

What would change if she told him the truth? Jim was part of the past and she wanted to look ahead.

"Because I knew I would be alone," was all she said. Then, as if to push the old memories behind her, she smiled at him.

Nick returned her smile, then ran his finger down her cheek as his expression grew serious. "I missed you," he said quietly. "I tried to stay away, but it was hard."

"Why did you think you had to stay away?"

Nick's eyes followed his finger as he traced the contours of her face. His expression was serious. "I felt I had no right. I felt as if I had overstepped the boundaries of my friendship with Jim."

Beth let that comment slip past her. Instead she wrapped her hand around Nick's wrist.

Nick cupped her face with his hand, his eyes boring into hers. "I care a lot about you, Beth. More than I've ever cared for anyone."

Beth's heart trembled at his words. She wanted so badly to tell him how she felt, but wasn't sure how to put her emotions into words that could so easily be misunderstood. Or ignored.

Instead she moved closer to him, slipped her other hand around his neck and drew his head down. Their lips met in a warm, gentle kiss. And in that kiss, she tried to express the emotion she couldn't capture in words.

She slipped her fingers through his hair as she drew back just enough to look into his eyes.

"What's happening, Beth? What's happening between us?" Nick's deep voice washed over her, his questions mimicking her own.

"I'm not sure," Beth whispered, afraid to voice her thoughts. She kissed him again, hoping he understood her actions.

"Bob said something interesting to me this

afternoon in the corral," Nick said, resting his chin on her hair. "He was talking about the ranch. And how he didn't have anyone to pass it on to. I wasn't sure if I heard him right, but he seems to be offering to help me buy it."

"Would you be interested?" Beth asked, hardly daring to think Nick was asking her opinion.

"I would be," Nick said quietly, pressing a light kiss to her hair. "If I had a good reason to."

"What would be a good reason?"

Nick said nothing for a moment. And in that moment Beth felt as if she hovered on a precipice. As if in that moment her life could go in one of two directions.

Off on her own as she had originally planned, or maybe, maybe…

"I have to think about it some more," Nick said.

"I can see you ranching," she said quietly. "You seem to enjoy working with the cows and you seem to love being here."

"I do." He kissed her again. "In many, many ways."

His words lingered and Beth once again felt a tremulous thrill.

Then he slipped his arm around her, pulling her close to him, holding her with one arm, and

Kyle with the other. Like the family she'd never imagined she would have. The family she would never have had with Jim.

She pushed his name back into the deep recesses of her mind. She had forgiven Jim. He was gone, and out of her life. Right now, right here, she was with Nick. For the first time in a long time she wasn't afraid to look into the future.

Because there was a strong possibility that in the future, Nick would be beside her.

Chapter Thirteen

Beth sat in the bedroom that Ellen had turned into a temporary crafting space. After the auction, Beth had been encouraged to make more cards, but she couldn't leave Kyle, so Nick, Ellen and Beth had moved what she needed into the old spare room so Beth could work in the main house.

She flipped through the patterned paper, a smile playing around the corners of her mouth. By the time Bob and Ellen came back from their visit, Nick had left.

Beth had retreated to Kyle's room with the excuse that she needed to feed him. She had let the feeding and changing and rocking to sleep stretch out, hoping to avoid Bob and Ellen. When she had finally come down, she escaped to her craft room with some murmured excuse about needing to make more cards.

It still puzzled her that Bob and Ellen seemed to be okay with the growing attraction between her and Nick. Surely it should be more difficult for them to see their daughter-in-law and grandchild connecting with someone else?

But she wasn't going to question too much. For now she had a job to do. Telling Ellen about the cards was true enough, but what she hadn't told her was who the cards were for.

Nick.

Earlier this evening words had tumbled and twisted through her mind, needing expression, but she was too afraid to tell him how she felt. What he meant to her.

Words, once spoken, once thrown into the air, could not be taken back. Words, spoken, could be misunderstood.

Hence the card and the message inside.

When Nick asked her why she didn't want to talk about Jim, she had found that she did. She wanted to tell Nick the truth, but not yet. Not while Jim meant so much to Nick.

Maybe later, she considered, smiling at the thought that there could be a "later" with Nick. That she wanted a "later" with Nick.

When she first met Jim at a party, he was full of life and promises that he would take her away from her dead-end job and show her the world. As the wife of a soldier, she did. Jim had been an escape from a life that she wanted to leave, but Nick was a gift. A blessing. She wanted to tell him all this and hoped her words conveyed her thoughts.

Twenty minutes later she reread her carefully scripted words inked with her favorite pen. As she glanced over them, she prayed Nick would understand what she was trying to say.

She slipped the card in the envelope but before she left, she checked on Kyle. He was still sleeping peacefully. Bob and Ellen were also asleep.

She glanced across the yard. Through the grove of trees, she could barely make out the shadow of Nick's house. She couldn't see any lights on. All the better.

So she carefully stole across the yard, thankful for the watery glow from the full moon hanging in the sky above, casting pale shadows on the shimmering snow.

Nick's house was quiet and she hesitated at the doorway, wondering if she dared go in.

She tapped the card against her thigh, biting her lip. Finally she pushed down her objections, carefully opened the door and stepped into the house. She glanced around, trying to think of the best place to put the envelope. The last time she'd given Nick a card, she'd put it on the kitchen table, but tonight she didn't dare venture too far into the house.

Then she saw the perfect spot. The stand where she and Jim had always put the car keys just inside the door.

Beth set the envelope on the stand where he would see it as he left. He couldn't miss it.

Quietly, she stepped back out of the house and walked across the yard, hugging herself against the cold. Before she walked around the grove of spruce trees hiding the two houses from each other, she shot another glance over her shoulder and sent up a prayer that Nick would understand what she wrote.

The ringing of the telephone broke into the silence of Sunday morning. Nick washed off the last bit of shaving lotion from his face and ran to answer it.

"Nick, could you do us a favor?" Ellen asked after greeting him. "Bob said you might be going to church this morning."

"Yes. I am." Yesterday, after he had listened to Bob read the Bible, he had come home and started reading it for himself. And as he read, he wondered if rebuilding a relationship with God meant he might be able to trust God with his burdens.

He had thought of Bob's invitation to come to church, so he had decided he would go. Now that Beth was going as well, he had an even greater incentive.

"That's great. Bob and I said we'd pick up Martha, the woman we visited last night, and take her to church this morning. We don't have enough room in the truck for her and Beth and Kyle, so would you mind bringing Beth and the baby to church this morning? She'd really like to go. You'll have to take our truck because the car seat is in it already," Ellen said, sounding as if it was a given that Nick would take Beth. "She'll be ready and waiting."

And with that she hung up.

Nick stared at the phone a moment, a thrill of anticipation overriding his own feeble objections.

Hope kindled the thought that maybe the kisses he and Beth had shared meant as much to her as they did to him. And maybe the moment they had shared at Ellen and Bob's last night showed Beth's state of mind more than her habitual reticence.

Nick pulled on a clean shirt and clean blue jeans. He didn't have a suit jacket or a tie. His leather coat would have to do.

He resisted the urge to stop in the bathroom

and check himself in the mirror again. He wasn't preening. He was going to church. With Beth.

Our souls are restless until they rest in You.

The quote from Augustine seemed to apply to his emotional state these days.

Nick still didn't know what to think of a God who could allow so much pain in the world, but he did know that since coming here, he'd felt that restlessness that Augustine had spoken of. That feeling of incompleteness he knew, intrinsically, could only be filled by God's presence.

Nick pulled his jacket off the coatrack and as he flipped it on, the phone rang again.

He walked over to answer it but just as he picked it up, the ringing stopped. Puzzled, he glanced at the call display. The number looked vaguely familiar, but where had he seen it before? Then he remembered the paper the mystery woman had given him at the fundraiser. He dug in his coat pocket. When he pulled it out he compared it to the number on the phone. It was the same.

He didn't have time nor the inclination to call the woman back. Beth was waiting for him.

He slipped the paper back into his coat pocket and hurried to the door.

Five inches of snow lay on the sidewalk and more fell in heavy flakes as he headed toward the other house. Yesterday Bob had talked about spring coming. Well, today it looked like full-blown winter again.

Nick pulled up the collar of his coat and carefully made his way through the heavy, wet snow up the walk to Bob and Ellen's house. He'd have to shovel the snow off here tomorrow. He stamped the snow off his boots on the step and lifted his hand to knock on the door but it opened right away.

"Don't stand there outside, come in," Ellen chided him. "Beth will be down right away."

Nick gave a curt nod of acknowledgment at her words, wishing his heart didn't jump in his chest. And then, there Beth was, wearing a pink turtleneck sweater and brown pants. The pink-and-brown scarf wrapped around her neck framed her face and set off her curly hair. Simple clothes but they made her look heartbreakingly beautiful.

"I hear you need a ride," he said, hoping he could sound more casual than he felt.

"If it doesn't work for you, it's okay." She fluttered her hands, glancing at Ellen as if for support.

"Of course it's okay," Ellen said. "We don't have enough room and you want to go to church. I'll get Kyle and you can get your coat on."

Ellen pulled a set of keys out of her purse and handed them to Nick. "Truck's in the garage."

"You trust me with it?" Nick joked.

"I trust you with my grandchild and daughter-in-law, the truck is peripheral." As Ellen gave him the keys, she caught his hand and squeezed. Nick looked down at her, puzzled.

Her gaze was steady and direct. "I mean that, Nick. I do trust you with Beth."

Nick thought back to last night. Ellen squeezed his hand again, as if underlining her comment. "You should probably go warm the truck up before you leave. I'll go get Kyle."

Then Ellen left, leaving Beth behind. She opened the closet and took her coat out. Nick took it and slipped it over her shoulders, feeling as if it was his right to do so. And as he did she gave him a smile that held a hint of a promise.

Ten minutes later he and Beth were driving down the road, snow slanting down toward them, the mountains hidden behind a bank of clouds. Beth hadn't said anything since they left the house and Nick tried to think of how to engage her in conversation. For now, all he could think about was sitting beside her in Bob and Ellen's living room, holding Kyle, pretending they might be a family.

"So, what made you decide to go to church?" he asked after a while, finally breaking the silence.

"It's been a while since I've been in church. I…I missed going."

Her admission surprised him. "I thought you and Jim attended." He shifted in his seat, glancing in the mirrors, checking for traffic. He had to turn the wipers on now and again to clear the windshield. The snow built up on the road and it looked as if the plows hadn't been out yet.

She shook her head. "Jim and I only went a few times. Mostly to satisfy his parents."

"Really." Nick was puzzled by that. Jim made it sound as if he and Beth went regularly. "Did you go before you and Jim dated?"

She waved off his question. "That was in the past. Doesn't matter anymore."

He had thought that after what they had shared, she would be more open.

However, at the same time he sensed pain simmering beneath her exterior.

"I got the impression that your family was a churchgoing one," he said, pressing the point.

"We were. And I often went until…" She let the sentence trail off.

"Until what."

"Doesn't matter."

She was making it clear she didn't want to talk about this and wanted him to leave her alone. He would have, but he thought of the kisses they had shared. The possibility that shimmered in her smile.

She held so much back and while it could be intriguing, lately it had grown exasperating. He kept waiting for her to open up, kept hoping that she would trust him with the secrets that hovered just behind her gaze.

"Until what, Beth?"

She turned to him. "Why do you want to know?"

He shot her a quick glance, then looked back at the road. "Because I think something is happening between us but at the same time I feel there are barriers." He wanted to know what was behind those barriers. He wanted to know if what they had was worth staying around for and fighting the guilt he constantly felt in her presence.

Beth pressed her lips together and for a moment Nick thought she wouldn't say anything.

"I...I stopped going to church after my dad left my mother when I was fourteen." Beth sighed as if the admission was too much for her.

"That was a long time ago."

"It was…" Her voice trailed off and he filled in the blanks.

"But it still bothers you."

Beth looked back at Kyle as if to make sure he was okay. "His leaving was difficult and made a huge difference in my life. My mother kind of shut off and shut me out after that."

"Did he ever tell you why he left?"

Beth rocked lightly in her seat. "The first I heard of him going was when I heard him arguing with my mother the night before he left." Beth stopped there and Nick waited, hoping she would say more.

"Then what happened?" Nick prompted, hoping that talking about her father would eventually get her around to talking about Jim.

Which, to him, would be a huge step down the path of healing. Which would erase one more barrier between them.

Beth was quiet a moment longer and he wondered if she would answer his question. "He left the house without saying goodbye. I heard him leaving and I ran after him, calling out his name. When I caught up to him, I hung on to his arm, asking him where he was going and if I could go with him." Beth stopped there, easing out a sigh. "Then he told me he was tired of being a father.

And because I was the only kid left at home, I could only assume he was tired of being *my* father. Then he turned around and kept walking. I pleaded with him to stay, but he kept going, as if I had said nothing." She released a bitter laugh. "I promised myself I would never run after any man again, which was a stupid promise in the end."

"Why do you say that?"

Beth didn't say anything and Nick fought down a beat of frustration. She said so little about Jim. He knew that part of her moving on had to involve talking about her husband, articulating her grief. And if she didn't move on, where would that leave her and him?

"I told you before, we don't need to talk about Jim," she said quietly.

Yet Jim hovered between them, a phantom he couldn't dismiss as long as she didn't talk about him. As long as Jim hovered in the background, so did Nick's guilt.

The farther they got from the ranch, the heavier the snow gathered on the highway. He slowed down a bit, adjusting to the conditions.

"So why are you going to church?" she prompted, changing the subject.

"There's an emptiness in me that I struggle

with. An emptiness that I know can only be filled with God."

"You stopped going to church?"

He nodded. "Losing my parents was hard. Being in Afghanistan only seemed to underline what I felt. That God didn't care."

"I used to think that, too," Beth murmured.

"I know I still struggle with the reality of what I saw in Afghanistan and the fact that God tells us He is in control," Nick said quietly, his thoughts veering from where he was now to where he was a few months ago. He wondered how his unit was doing. What was happening?

"I'm sure it was hard," she said.

"It was for me. Jim always had a more positive attitude about everything. He always said that what we were doing made a difference, one trip at a time. I clung to that, even though there were times I didn't believe it."

"And now? Do you believe that what you did was important?"

Nick nodded. "I do. I learned a lot from Jim that way."

"Your conversation always seems to come back to Jim."

"I think we need to talk about him."

"Why?"

"Because I feel, at times, like he's still between us."

"Us? Is there an us?"

Nick shot her a quick glance, then looked back at the road. "Why don't you tell me?"

"I think so," she said quietly. "I want to think so."

Nick's heart jumped at her admission. It wasn't much, but for her, so quiet and contained, it was everything.

"But I don't want to talk about Jim. Not yet."

"Why not?" Nick asked, feeling as if they had simply circled back to the very thing he felt was an impediment to their relationship. "Why can't you or won't you talk about Jim?"

Beth sighed softly, looking ahead at the snow gathering on the hood of the truck. "You and I have a different version of Jim and the relationship he and I had," she said. "You keep saying how thinking about our relationship kept you going at times. That thinking about it gave you hope." She sighed again. "It doesn't matter anymore and I don't know if I need to disillusion you right now."

"What? Disillusion me?"

He wanted to know more, but the truck's back tire slipped. Nick's heart jumped and he turned his attention back to his driving. Then the truck fishtailed and Nick corrected, adrenaline surging through him.

What was the matter with him? He'd driven on snowy roads before. He'd driven in dust storms. He'd driven while being shot at. Why was this making him so antsy?

Because he had Beth and Kyle with him. Because these two people were counting on him to get them to church in one piece. Safe. Alive.

Because Beth had said their might be an "us" and if that was the case, he needed more than ever to make sure they would stay safe. Beth and Kyle were counting on him to protect them.

The truck fishtailed again and Nick caught it in time to hear Beth's sudden cry of warning.

A vehicle came toward them, headed straight for the truck.

Beth stifled a scream.

He had to make a split-second decision. Move right to the ditch, or left to the wrong side of the road.

The other car kept coming. Nick turned left and stepped on the gas. The truck's tires spun uselessly on the snow and still the other vehicle came toward them.

Please, Lord, he prayed. *Let me get out of this*

mess. His mind flashed back to another prayer. One that hadn't been answered.

He kept pressing on the gas, kept praying his vehicle would respond and change direction and suddenly, at the last second, his truck swerved to the other side of the road, missing the approaching vehicle by inches.

But Nick no longer had control of the truck and it rocketed forward. Straight into the ditch.

Snow flew up and over the truck, covering the windshield as they crashed to an abrupt halt.

Nick's hands were like ice, his heart pounding in his chest with the force of a sledgehammer. He shot a panicked glance over at Beth who stared at him, her eyes wide with fright.

A trickle of blood drifted out of the side of her mouth.

Nick was out of his seat belt and across the cab, his hands cradling her face before he even realized he had done so.

"Look at me. Beth. Look at me." His voice shook and his hands trembled as his fingers traced her face and explored her head, searching for the source of the blood, his heart clenched in fear. "What happened? Where are you hurt?"

"I'm okay," she said, lifting her hand to her head.

Her eyes held his and she gave him a tremulous smile.

"I need to call an ambulance." Where was his cell phone? Why couldn't he find his phone?

She caught his hands, stopping him. "Nick. I'm fine. I just bit my lip. That's all. Look." She pulled her lip down with her finger and then he saw where the blood was coming from. "It's nothing serious."

His heart slowed, but his sense of responsibility intensified. "I'm sorry, Beth. I'm so sorry. I should have been more careful."

"It wasn't your fault. If you hadn't ditched the truck we could have hit that other vehicle."

Nick took a steadying breath, unable to look away from Beth, still not convinced nothing worse had happened than a tiny cut in her lip. He gently smoothed the blood away with his thumb, wanting to erase the evidence of what had just happened.

So close. So close. Why hadn't he paid closer attention? They'd come within inches of hitting that other truck.

In spite of what Beth said, had he done things differently, they wouldn't have hit the ditch. "How's Kyle?" he asked, pulling away, dragging his shaking hands over his face.

Beth unbuckled her seat belt and leaned over the baby seat. "He's sleeping."

Beth sat back, drawing in another breath, belying her easy dismissal of what happened, then jumped just as Nick heard a knocking on his window. He looked over to see a man wearing a down-filled jacket, toque and huge grin motioning for Nick to roll his window down.

"Hey, I just saw what happened," the man said. "Can't believe that other guy just kept on going. What a loser. I can pull you out. You got a tow rope?"

Nick glanced over his shoulder. A large, four-wheel drive truck stood parked on the highway behind him, its exhaust pluming into the cold air.

He pulled himself together to focus on the job at hand. "I'm sure there's one in the jockey box," Nick said as he got out of the truck.

"Let's get it hooked up and get you and your wife back on your way again."

Nick didn't bother correcting him. He just wanted to get the truck out of the ditch and Beth and Kyle somewhere safe. He found the rope in the box as he predicted.

"Nasty driving weather, ain't it?" The man huffed as he worked his way up the steep embankment to his truck, dragging the tow rope behind him through the snow. "Makes you wonder if you shouldn't stay at home 'stead of risking your life on these roads. Looks like you folks were headed for church, so we'll get you on your way and you can go and thank God He sent me your way." The man laughed at his own joke. "You also might want to get to town and see about getting new tires on that truck. Those all-season radials just don't cut it in this weather. Might want to think about that, especially if you got a wife and kid to think about. Can't be too careful."

Nick didn't bother replying as the man chatted on about the weather and tires and responsible driving, each word driving a stake of guilt into Nick's heart.

After much digging and some swearing on the part of their rescuer, they had the snow cleared away from the hitch on Nick's truck and the tow rope hooked up. Nick got back into the truck, put it in Reverse and waited until the rope was taut, then hit the accelerator.

Tires whined, snow spun and the truck veered to the right, but a few seconds later the truck came up on the pavement and the rope between the two trucks grew slack. They were out.

Nick walked around his truck, checking for

damage, but other than some snow packed in the wheel wells, the vehicle was fine. There wasn't even a dent in the body.

"I tell you, mister," their rescuer said as he unhooked the rope and began coiling it up. "You'll want to get better tires on that truck."

"Thanks for the tow. What do I owe you?" Nick asked, pulling out his wallet.

"Nothing. Just get the missus and kid safely to your destination and we'll call it even," the man said with another grin. He pitched the rope in the back of Nick's truck. "You're lucky," he said, looking over the truck. "Lucky that nothing worse happened."

He gave Nick a wave, got in his own truck and drove off.

Nick gave his nerves a few moments to settle down and the trembling in his hands to ease. Then he got back in the truck and glanced over his shoulder. All clear. He pulled in a long, slow breath, glanced at Beth as if to make sure she was okay, then pulled back onto the road.

"Do you still want to go to church?" he asked. "We're going to be late."

"I really want to," Beth said.

Nick wasn't sure he could concentrate on the minister after this, but he agreed to go.

The drive to church was quiet and slow. Nick replayed the scene over and over in his head. So many things could have happened it made his stomach roil. The Good Samaritan who had helped them hadn't come right out and said it, but Nick felt as if the accident was his fault. Did he have any right with the responsibility of Beth and Kyle? Was he really to be trusted as Ellen had said?

Chapter Fourteen

Thankfully the snow had eased off when they got to church and in the distance Nick saw patches of blue sky between the clouds.

Nick scanned the full parking lot and with a flicker of dismay noticed that Bob and Ellen weren't here yet. What was he going to do? He certainly wouldn't be driving Beth and Kyle back to the ranch.

Beth took Kyle out of his car seat and slung a diaper bag over her shoulder.

"Do you want some help?" Nick asked.

"No. I'm fine."

Of course she didn't need his help.

Thankfully people were still milling about so the church service hadn't started, though singing was coming from the sanctuary.

Nick followed Beth up the stairs, surprised at

how weak his knees felt. Reaction, he thought, remembering all too well how long it could take before the shakes went away and confidence returned after some of the more difficult trips.

They walked in and found an empty space then sat down. Nick pulled in another breath, leaning forward, his elbows resting on his knees.

"You look a little pale," Beth said.

"I'm fine." He gave her a quick smile, then looked away, wishing that Bob and Ellen were here. He couldn't think about the drive back home.

"You don't look okay," Beth said.

"You're the one with a split lip," Nick said, his eyes going to her mouth.

"I bit my lip because I was nervous. I was just being silly." She laid her hand on his shoulder and for a moment Nick felt assured.

Thankfully he didn't need to say anything more because the worship group announced a song and the congregation rose to their feet to sing.

As the service went through the liturgy, his confidence returned. At the same time he struggled to pay attention, fighting the distraction of Beth beside him. He was here because of a hunger to worship God and a need to find his way past the guilt that grew stronger each day instead of easing away.

Hitting the ditch on the way to church with Beth and Kyle in the truck hadn't helped him try to take a vacation from his guilt trip.

It wasn't your fault. You had no choice.

But even as he thought that, he wondered if he could have avoided it. Done something different. Taken a different route. His mind spiraled back to those gut-clenching moments after the accident with Jim when he had wondered repeatedly what would have happened had he not listened to Jim and traded places. Should he have insisted Jim drive as he had been commanded to? He hadn't relived those moments in months, but now, in church, they were as clear as if they had happened seconds ago.

The pastor started speaking, pulling Nick back to the present.

They were asked to open their Bibles and turn to Psalm 121. This was followed by a general rustling of pages and then an almost holy silence.

"'I lift up my eyes to the hills—where does my help come from?'" the pastor read. "'My help comes from the Lord, the Maker of heaven and earth. He will not let your foot slip—He who watches over you will not slumber…'"

As the minister read Nick thought of the mountains of Afghanistan and how often his eyes would lift up to the hills watching for enemies. Watching for trouble.

He thought about how Jim, who was supposed to be watching out, fell asleep and Jim wasn't watching anymore.

Nick wanted to stop the images flashing through his mind as he sat beside Jim's widow, but it was as if hitting the ditch just a few minutes before had dislodged old memories loose.

"'…the Lord will watch over your coming and going both now and forevermore.'"

Nick pulled his attention back to the passage in front of him, willing the pictures and the accompanying guilt away.

The minister closed the Bible and began to speak. Nick kept his eyes on the book still open in his hands as he read and reread the Psalm, seeking comfort and absolution.

The Lord will watch over your coming and going both now and forevermore.

And what about the coming and going of the people he was supposed to take care of? The people who relied on him?

"…what this Psalm teaches us is not that as Christians, we won't face trouble—our foot slipping, being smitten by the sun by day nor the moon at night." Nick's attention was pulled back by the words of the preacher. "Not that we'll never make mistakes, but that as Christians, we can be assured that the God of all heaven and earth, as opposed to the gods that the people of Israel were surrounded with, would never lose interest in us. God is bigger than the things that overwhelm our lives and He promises rest for our troubled, weary and guilt-ridden souls that is far beyond any help or rest we can receive from anything on this earth. Believing in God doesn't give us tools to protect ourselves or our loved ones from evil or pain or sorrow, but we can know that in all the things that happen to us God is beside us, before us, behind us, within us."

Nick clung to the words of the message as he tried to imagine a life free from the guilt he struggled with. He glanced at Beth. In spite of what the pastor said, he wanted to protect Beth from evil, pain and sorrow. He had thought to protect Jim, but couldn't. Did that mean God didn't care?

Beth caught his gaze, gave him a careful smile and his troubled heart beat just a little harder.

He'd spent so much of his life just going through the motions, following orders, letting other people decide where he would go and what he would do. Now he was on his own and this beautiful woman made him think about possibilities and, for the first time in a long time, about a future.

And what the pastor had just talked about gave him a hope for that future.

Please, Lord, he prayed as he returned Beth's smile, *show me what I have to do with my guilt. I don't know how to carry it anymore. I don't want Jim to come between me and Beth anymore.*

He turned away from Beth, waiting, as if here, in church, he could hear God better, struggling to hear the words of absolution his soul needed so badly. But all he heard was the rustling of the congregation as they rose to sing the song of response to the sermon.

The worship band had been replaced by an organist who let the introductory chords of the song resound through the sanctuary.

Nick recognized the song. He took the other half of the hymnal that Beth held out to him and sang along.

"'A mighty fortress is our God. A bulwark never failing. Our helper He, amid the flood, of mortal ills prevailing.'"

As Nick sang, he felt a peculiar notion that the song was speaking some message he couldn't decipher.

"'...the body they may kill, God's truth abideth still. His kingdom is forever.'"

When the song was done, the minister sent them out with a final blessing. Nick tried to capture the fleeting emotion he had experienced while singing the song, but it was gone.

He looked around for Beth, but she already stood in the aisle. He saw her talking with Trina, the woman she had been chatting with at the fundraiser. She was smiling and looking animated. She looked busy so Nick walked the other way, looking for Ellen and Bob.

Out in the foyer, he lost track of Beth but then he heard Ellen calling out.

"Nick, there you are. How did everything go?"

His heart did a slow turn, as the events prior to church services slammed back into his mind and with them, an extra measure of guilt.

He turned to face Ellen, wondering how to tell her then decided to get directly to the point. "I hit the ditch."

Ellen's eyes grew wide and her hand flew to her open mouth. "Is everything okay? Is Beth okay and Kyle?"

"Beth and Kyle are fine." He blew out a sigh.

"I'd prefer it if you drove her and Kyle home. I'll move the car seat to your vehicle."

"That's not necessary," Ellen protested. "I'm sure Beth would prefer to go back with you. Why don't you drive her back in our vehicle?"

He would have preferred to go back with Beth as well, but he shook his head.

"It is necessary. Please. I'm not comfortable with that kind of responsibility right now. Not after what happened. And I don't want you or Bob driving that truck back, either."

Ellen frowned, but nodded her agreement. "You look a little pale."

"I'm okay." He gave her a curt nod. "I'll move the car seat, then see you back at the house."

"Are you coming for lunch?"

Nick held that thought a moment. He was about to say yes when Ellen's eyes narrowed just as he felt a hand on his arm.

He turned and came face-to-face with Mrs. Cruikshank, the woman who had made some disparaging comments to Beth at the fundraiser.

He gave her a tight smile. "What can I do for you?"

Mrs. Cruikshank looked pointedly at Ellen who shrugged but took the unspoken hint and walked away.

"I understand you served with Jim in Afghanistan," she said, raising one perfectly plucked eyebrow.

"I did." What did the mother of Beth's former boss want with him?

"I know this because Shellie, my daughter, and Jim…they corresponded."

"And?" Nick shifted his weight on his feet. He really wanted to go back home. To clear his already troubled mind.

To see Beth again. To see if she still trusted him after what happened this morning.

And he did not want to talk about Jim and Afghanistan right about now.

"I understand my daughter, Shellie, has been trying to contact you. She gave you her number at the fundraiser but you haven't called her back."

Nick struggled to put this all together.

"We're going to be moving away from town in a few weeks and she needs to speak with you before we go."

"I couldn't imagine what I can tell her that she doesn't already know," Nick said.

"She's waiting outside." Mrs. Cruikshank caught Nick by the arm. "Please, please talk to her. She needs closure and she's not going to find it until she talks to you."

Nick sighed. He wanted closure, too, but it didn't look as if that was coming his way anytime soon. If he could give this Shellie something, maybe it would chase away some of his own demons.

"Okay. I'll talk to her." He headed toward the exit that Mrs. Cruikshank had pointed to.

He went through the doors and found himself in a small courtyard protected on three sides. On a bench, in the courtyard, sat Shellie.

She looked up when the door fell shut behind him and she shot to her feet.

"You didn't call me," she said, her voice a strangled sound.

Nick shook his head. "No. I'm sorry. I was busy." And he'd had no desire to talk to another woman, not when Beth took up so much of his mind. "I understand you want to talk to me about Jim. Why?"

Shellie looked at him, her eyes red and glistening. "I went to school with Jim. He was a dear friend. I just want to know if he ever said anything about me."

Nick dug through his memories but came up empty. "No. Sorry."

She stared at him as if she didn't believe him. "How could he not? Jim told me all about you.

How you were raised on a ranch. Like him. How you lost your parents."

Nick looked at her again, trying to dredge up any memory of her or her face.

"Sorry. Jim only ever talked about Beth and only ever had pictures up of Beth."

"Of course he did. Jim liked making a good impression." Shellie pressed her lips together, her gloved fingertips resting against her mouth, not saying anything more after her enigmatic comment. He waited a moment, watching the snow falling and catching on her auburn hair and thick eyelashes. She drew in a long breath.

"How did he die?" she finally asked.

Nick sighed. "It doesn't matter."

"It does to me. I need to know."

She looked as if she was on the verge of breaking down. He highly doubted she was in any position to hear what he had to say.

"Was he shot?" she asked, her voice rising on the question. "Was it a road bomb? A suicide bomber? Jim used to tell me that if he died, he hoped it would be quick, and I need to know if it was quick."

"How would you know what he said?"

"We wrote each other," she said. "Lots. He was more than just a friend."

Nick doubted that. Jim had never even mentioned this woman's name, but he wasn't going to argue with a woman on the verge of hysteria.

"He told me all about you," she said, a defensive tone in her voice. "He told me you hated driving. He told me that you always wore a silver cross that you got from your father and every time you'd get into the truck, you'd hold on to it for a few seconds."

"How did you know that?" Jim used to tease him about being superstitious and/or religious, depending on Jim's mood, but only Jim had ever seen him do that.

"He told me because we wrote each other, chatted with each other on the computer. He was everything to me. Now I have nothing," she continued. "I don't even know what happened to him in the end."

Nick shoved his hand through his snow-dampened hair, trying to fit this woman's story into what he knew of his buddy who only ever talked about Beth. Who only carried pictures of Beth.

Shellie came closer to him, her expression so full of sorrow that in spite of his disbelief in her story, it touched his heart.

"Please tell me what happened. Please." Her

breath came out in a cloud of fog and her eyes sparkled with unshed tears.

Nick struggled with his own thoughts and memories, surprised in one way that she would ask. Not even Beth or Ellen or Bob had ever asked the details of that day.

Details that had come flooding back after he hit the ditch just this morning. Details he didn't want to talk about because the memories accused.

"Tell me. Please."

The pleading note in her voice seemed to dislodge the words and memories so recently unearthed by the accident of the morning. It was as if he had to speak them to get them out of his mind. He couldn't tell Beth because she never wanted to talk about Jim.

"A sniper shot him." The words slipped out and once they started, it was as if he couldn't stop. "Usually I watched out and he drove. I didn't like driving as much as he did, but he had been up late the night before—"

"We were talking on Skype," Shellie interrupted.

"—so I drove," Nick said, letting her comment slip by him. "He was supposed to watch out, but he was tired and fell asleep. He wasn't paying attention and he got shot." Nick curled his hands into fists.

"You couldn't save him? Why couldn't you save him?"

Nick couldn't say anything, his own memories threatening to swamp him.

"If he was driving like he was supposed to, then it would have been you that was shot."

Her accusation struck a direct hit on his own guilt. This guilt was the very thing he struggled with from the minute he heard the crack of the rifle and saw Jim slump down on the seat beside him. Then everything went haywire. In the moment he looked over at Jim, the truck hit a hole the other vehicles had avoided and Nick's truck rolled out of control. By the time they got Jim out, he was breathing his last breath.

"If he had been driving he wouldn't have been shot," Shellie said.

Her words gave voice to his own remorse and constant regret.

"You should have been the one that died," she said, taking a step closer, her hands clenched into white-knuckled fists. "You killed him," she sobbed. "You killed him." Then she turned around and ran away, snow swirling around her.

Nick dropped onto the bench, shoved his hands

through his hair, his thoughts a roaring, blinding storm of accusation.

He had killed Jim.

If it wasn't for him, Jim would be alive.

He had killed Jim and this morning he had almost killed Jim's wife and child.

He had no right to be here. No right to be with Beth.

He had to leave.

Chapter Fifteen

Beth dropped the book she'd been trying to read on the end table, got up and walked to the living-room window. Lunchtime had come and gone, but Nick hadn't shown up though she knew Ellen had invited him.

Had he read her card? Had he found it? He hadn't said anything about it this morning so she assumed he had missed it. Surely, by now, he would have seen it.

An icy fist clutched her heart. Maybe he *had* read it and that was why he stayed away. Maybe she had said too much and had scared him off.

Bob looked up from the book he was reading, smiling at her. "You want to go out for a walk? Ellen and I can babysit."

Beth bit her lip, wondering what to do. She was tired of pacing around, restless, unsure. In the past few days, Beth had let a slim hope burn in her soul. The hope that Nick and her had a future. That she and Nick could stay. Here. With Bob and Ellen.

When he didn't come to lunch that hope had been diminished.

"If you don't mind," she said, feeling a need to get out. "Kyle is sleeping and I won't go far."

"We'll manage if he wakes up, but I think he'll be fine," Ellen said, looking up from the sweater she was knitting. Beth knew it was for Kyle, as was the blanket she had just finished the other day.

Ellen's love for Kyle was all-encompassing, gentle and fierce at the same time. Beth felt a flicker of remorse when she thought of her erstwhile plans. Plans she had put on hold in the past few days.

And now?

Beth spun around and strode to the porch.

She threw on her coat, grabbed a toque and mitts and as she stepped out of the house she slipped them on. The sun hid behind clouds scudding across the sky, remnants of the snowstorm of this morning. Beth shivered, recalling her fear when she saw that car barreling toward them.

But Nick had saved them. Sure he had hit the ditch, but what else could he do? He had saved their lives.

She walked far enough so she could see the other house, but saw no sign of life there. Did she dare go over there? And say what?

Fear clutched her midsection. Had she done it again? Had she poured out her heart only to have it ignored?

She couldn't believe Nick would do that.

Then why is he staying away?

The sound of a vehicle's engine broke the silence and Beth frowned as she glanced down the driveway. Bob and Ellen hadn't said anything about visitors.

A car came around the last bend in the driveway. As it drove toward her, Beth noticed the plastic rectangle on the roof of the car and the logo on the door. Harrison's Cab Service? What was a cab doing all the way out here?

A hard shiver seized her body and she felt a hollow ache in her chest.

The last time she'd seen a cab here was when Nick arrived.

The car pulled up to Nick's house and stopped. The cab driver knew exactly where he had to be. Nick must have given him specific instructions.

She heard the sound of a door closing and Nick came out of her old house, his duffel bag slung over his shoulder, carrying another bag in his other hand.

He limped toward the cab, his head down, as if concentrating on every step he took away from the house.

As she watched him, images from her past mocked her. Her father leaving her. Jim leaving to go be with another woman.

Now Nick was leaving.

You have to stop him.

The voice reverberated through her mind, and she shoved it aside. She wasn't chasing a man again. Ever.

So she stood her ground and waited, her hope a vague wisp that couldn't be grasped.

Nick raised his head and saw her. He stopped and their gazes met across the distance between them.

Weariness was etched into his face and in his eyes she saw a dull pain. What had happened to him since the last time she saw him?

"Hey, Beth," was all he said, letting his duffel bag fall to the ground beside the cab.

As he walked toward her she swallowed down a knot of panic, sliding her bunched fists into the pocket of her coat. "Are you going?" she asked when he came closer.

Nick gave her a curt nod, still holding her gaze.

"Why?" She could barely formulate the question through lips tight with fear.

Nick's sigh came out in a cloud of vapor. He pulled his hand over his face and shook his head. "I can't be what you need, Beth. I can't take care of you."

"I don't need you to take care of me," she said. "I just…" She wanted to say "need you" but she had said so much in her card, what more could she add? If that didn't convince him, her feeble words couldn't.

"I can't be the man Jim was," Nick said. "I can't protect you and take care of you."

"Why are you talking like that?" Her confusion grew with every word he spoke. "Why are you comparing yourself to Jim?" Especially when he was everything Jim never was. Faithful. Loving. Responsible. Helpful. Unselfish.

"I'm not supposed to be here," Nick said.

"I don't understand what you are trying to tell me," Beth cried. "Why are you saying this?"

Nick took another step closer to her, his eyes narrowed with…anger?

"I'm not supposed to be here because I was supposed to be sitting where Jim was the day he got shot. That bullet was meant for me, not him." Nick spat out the words as if they were distasteful for him. "I was supposed to be watching out instead of driving. Those were the orders. But Jim was tired so I drove. He'd been up the night before talking on Skype, so I drove. And because I drove, he caught the bullet. He died when it should have been me."

"So if you hadn't been driving—"

"Jim would have been driving and he would still be alive."

She blinked, trying to absorb this information.

"Don't you get it, Beth? I'm the reason Jim is dead." Nick almost shouted the words.

"I thought a sniper killed him."

"Yes."

"So…why are you saying that you killed him?" She was struggling to understand Nick's anger.

"You need to know what kind of man I am."

Beth frowned. "I know what kind of man you are."

"I was supposed to have died," Nick said. "Not Jim. If things had gone the way they should, like I said, I would have been shot. And Jim would be here. With you."

Beth slowly realized what he was saying. "Why are you taking this burden on?"

"Doesn't this matter? Don't you care?" Nick asked.

Beth stared at him, stunned by his anger and at the same time, the pleading note in his voice.

"I don't know how I'm supposed to react," Beth said, struggling to find her way through this maze of emotions. "If he had been at the wheel, maybe he would have driven faster. Maybe the shooter would have missed or got someone else. Anything else could have happened."

"But Jim died."

His words were short. Sharp. As if by saying them he was trying to hurt her. To shock her into saying something or doing something.

She wasn't sure what he wanted from her. "I'm not bitter about Jim's death, Nick." It was all she could give him right now.

"So you don't think it's my fault?"

"No. Of course not." She looked at him, wishing she knew what to say to take his guilt away. But again, she didn't want to talk about Jim. She had other things on her mind. "So where does that leave us?"

"Us?" He gave a short laugh. "Do you really think there can be an 'us'? After what I told you?"

These words hurt much more than anything else he had said.

"*Us* was a dream, a fantasy," he continued, his

voice harsh and bitter. "It was never meant to be. I can't be the same man Jim was. I can't take care of you. I can't protect you."

"Jim never protected me in his life."

"Of course he did. He loved you."

Beth's shame over Jim's actions was brushed away by her need to make Nick understand and by a deep-seated fear that Nick was leaving. She had to tell him the truth.

She drew a long, slow breath, reminding herself that she had forgiven Jim. Now Nick needed to know the truth.

"Jim was a womanizer who cheated on me more times than he was faithful to me," she said, forcing the words past her shame. Too much was at stake here. She needed to let Nick know the truth. "I don't know why he thought he felt he had to lie to you about our relationship, but it wasn't perfect, that's for sure. In fact, I was going to leave him, divorce him, but I wanted to wait until he was back from overseas to tell him."

Nick simply stared at her, as if trying to mesh what he'd heard from Jim with what she told him.

"I found text messages on his phone from a girl-friend," she said, trying to make him see. "They had been carrying on ever since he came back here. I found out shortly after I got pregnant. And I got pregnant because I mistakenly believed Jim would be the faithful husband he promised me he'd be."

"Who was the girl?"

Beth sliced the air with her hand. "Doesn't matter. I don't care who she was. It just matters that Jim lied to me. And he lied to you. I know I'm not supposed to speak ill of the dead, but he was a lying cheater. His death was hard. It was sad. But for me, truthfully, it was a relief."

Nick looked away, shoving his hand through his hair. "I don't…I don't understand."

"Of course not. For some reason of his own, Jim made you believe something untrue. A fantasy that didn't exist."

Nick looked up at her, his eyes narrowed with confusion. "Why didn't you tell me this before?"

"I couldn't." She waited, trying to find words to convey her feelings. "I couldn't at first because of shame and I didn't want Bob and Ellen to find out. Then I couldn't because I didn't want to destroy your dream. And for a small moment, I thought maybe Jim had changed."

Nick glanced at the cab, still waiting. The driver pointed at the meter, reminding Nick that time and money was ticking.

Beth took a step back, as if giving him space. If he needed to leave, then she wouldn't stop him.

"You say you feel guilty about Jim's death, but didn't you listen to the minister this morning? He told us that God is bigger than the things that overwhelm us and though we're not guaranteed we won't have any troubles, we can know God is around us. I really thought that was a comfort, didn't you?"

Nick's slow nod was a bit of a comfort to her, as well.

Then Nick sighed and looked up at her. "I need to know where Jim is in your life now."

Beth held his question a moment in her mind, testing her emotions. "Jim is buried. Gone. Jim has not been a part of my life or my plans since he left for Afghanistan."

Nick glanced at the cabbie, then at her again. "What about me? Am I a part of your life?"

Beth hid her hurt and took a chance. "How can you think you're not?" She spoke the words quietly, not trusting them to convey the power of her emotions. How much he meant to her.

"I can think that because you never say anything to me. You tell me nothing."

Beth hesitated again. "You always wanted to talk about Jim. And like I told you, I couldn't talk about him. I didn't want to talk about him. I...I wanted to talk about you. Me. Us." She spoke her last word so quietly, she doubted he heard it.

Nick closed the distance between them, looking at her, his blue eyes boring into hers. "Give me a reason to stay, Beth. Tell me why I shouldn't get into that cab."

"Didn't you read my card?"

"The thank-you card?" Nick looked genuinely puzzled.

"No, the one I left on the table in the porch."

He shook his head and suddenly things became a bit clearer.

"Stay there," she said, raising her hand in a warning gesture. "Don't leave until I get back."

The heavy snow slowed her down and she floundered, trying to find her footing.

He's going to leave.

Beth pushed the thought aside and burst into the house. She glanced at the table but didn't see the card. What happened? She went farther into the house and then she saw the corner of the envelope on the floor. It must have fallen.

She snatched the card and straightened. And stopped.

You told yourself you were never going to run after another man again. If Nick cares, then the card won't matter. If he doesn't care...again, the card won't matter.

She looked down at the card and all it represented to her. Inside the envelope were words she had never dared speak to anyone before.

Drawing in a long, slow breath, she lowered her head, praying for strength and wisdom.

She heard the horn of the cab honk once. Twice.

Her heart hammered in her chest. What should she do?

Go after him. He's worth it, she thought.

Beth spun around just as she heard the sound of the cab leaving. Her hand reached for the door and she glanced out the side window of the entrance in time to see the cab heading back down the driveway.

Too late. Nick was gone.

Beth clutched the card and yanked open the door. This was unacceptable. He didn't even wait to see what she had to say. Well, she would show him. Maybe he thought he could just leave without things being resolved between them, but she wouldn't let that happen. She was going after him.

She ran out the door, snow kicking up behind

her. She'd take one of Bob's trucks. She'd follow him…where? Maybe the airport in Calgary.

She looked up and then skidded to a halt.

Nick still stood in the middle of the yard, his shoulders hunched against the cool wind drifting down from the mountains. His duffel bag lay in the snow beside him. And he looked directly at her.

Pulling in a steadying breath, Beth walked toward him, her card still in her hand. She stopped in front of him and handed it to him.

Nick looked down at the card, then up at her, tapping it against his other hand. "Why don't you tell me what's in here?"

Her first instinct was to pull back. To retreat. Putting her thoughts into words meant opening herself up to misunderstanding. It meant making herself vulnerable. "I don't know if I can."

"I'm not your father, Beth, and you already told me, I'm not Jim."

She knew this meant he would stay. He would listen. Yet it was difficult to open up after being silent for so long.

"I'm still here, Beth, and I need to hear what you have to say. I need to hear you speak it. I'm all alone here and I'm afraid, too. But I like to believe that we can trust each other."

He reached out and touched her arm, as if to encourage her.

Swallowing down her fear, winging up a prayer for strength, she took the card again, her voice a tremulous sound in the vast emptiness of the yard.

"I thanked you for being a strength to me. For being a support. For being beside me when you didn't have to be." She handed him the card, looking into his blue eyes now shining with a light she couldn't identify. "I told you what you meant to me. That I trust you with my life and that I trust you with my son's life." She gave him a quick smile. "Like I did this morning in spite of how you saw the situation. I trust you, Nick. But more than that…I…I love you."

Nick shoved the card into his pocket, then closing the distance between them, swept her into his arms. He held her close, his head buried against her neck, his arms wrapped tightly around her. "Oh, Beth, I don't deserve your words, but I treasure them. And I treasure you." He drew back just enough to find her mouth with his. After a time he pulled back, raising one hand to brush an errant tear from her cheek. His eyes traveled over her face as if studying it. "I love you so much, Beth. I've never felt like this before. Ever."

Beth felt another tear slide down her cheek but she let it go. She caught his face in her hands and dropped another kiss on his mouth. "You know you talk about protecting me but that's a hard thing to do," she said. "Know this, Nick Colter. You may not be able to protect me from all the bad things in life, but I know and I feel that you will always protect my heart."

Nick shook his head and pulled her close one more time. Then he brushed her hair back from her face and smiled down at her. "We have to go talk to Bob and Ellen. Before we do, though, I'd like to have a look at this, if it's okay with you?" Nick pulled the card out of his pocket and cocked a questioning eyebrow at Beth.

She nodded, taking a step back as if to give him space. He carefully opened the envelope and pulled the card out. "This is cool," he said, touching the metallic paper she had used for the front of the card. The few moments he took to look at it warmed Beth's soul. How blessed was she to be with someone who knew what was important to her?

He opened it and started reading. His light frown was replaced with a gentle smile. When he was done, he paused a moment, then looked up at her. "Thanks, Beth. I don't deserve this."

"I think you do." She gave him a gentle smile.

"Hey, you two, what are you doing out there?" Ellen's voice called across the yard.

Nick picked up his duffel bag and slung it over his shoulder as Beth picked up his other bag. Then he took her hand.

"Well, Beth, for better or for worse, at least we have each other."

"Let's go talk to them," Beth agreed, clinging to his hand, to his strength.

Together they walked to the house.

"I know this will be difficult to understand and most likely accept, but Beth and I love each other," Nick said, leaning forward and holding Beth's hand in his. He thought his hands were cold, but hers were like ice. He knew this would be hard for her. Ellen and Bob treated her like they would their own flesh and blood daughter.

They sat in the living room facing Bob and Ellen who sat in their respective chairs.

"When I first came here I didn't come to make a move on my friend's wife—" here Nick shot an apologetic glance at Beth "—but what happened between us just, well, happened. I don't expect you to understand, but we thought we should let you know."

Ellen's gaze was firmly fixed on her clasped

hands and Bob leaned back in his chair, his arms folded over his chest, his lips pursed as if thinking.

Nick pressed his lips together, shooting Beth an encouraging glance and a quick smile.

"I would be lying if I said that I didn't see this coming," Ellen said quietly, weaving and unweaving her fingers. "I guessed that night I had to go away that something important had happened between you." Her voice cracked with emotion and Nick felt as if the burden he thought he could put down lay beside him, ready to be shouldered again. Guilt. The very nerve of sorrow. And in spite of what Beth had said about Jim, his death had still brought sorrow to this household.

Ellen reached up and surreptitiously wiped her eyes, then she sniffed and looked up at both of them. Her smile trembled over her lips, but it was a smile.

"As a mother, it's hard to see a child heartbroken, and as a mother, I always want to fix, to rectify, to honor any request. Beth, you're like a daughter to me and…" Ellen's voice wavered again as she shot a glance over at Bob. "And I know my son wasn't always the husband he should be. Both Bob and I have guessed at that for some time. We've known for sure for only a few weeks."

Nick frowned, trying to understand what Ellen was saying.

Bob leaned forward. "We know about Shellie, Beth. We heard from a couple of different people."

This time it was Beth's turn to frown. "Shellie? What are you saying?"

Bob shot a panicked look at Ellen, who took over.

"I found out a few weeks ago that Martha had seen Shellie and Jim in a restaurant in Calgary, just before he left for Afghanistan. They looked, well, intimate." Ellen heaved out a heavy sigh, turning to Beth. "I suspected that something was going on, but I never knew for sure, and you seemed to be unaware so I decided it would be best to keep quiet. When Jim died and when we saw you didn't grieve the same way, I wondered why. When I found out about Shellie, I knew."

Beth nodded, still frowning, looking as if she was struggling to put everything together. "Jim and Shellie?"

Ellen drew in a deep, pain-filled breath. "Had this happened before? Had Jim cheated on you before? Or was Shellie the only one?"

Beth squeezed Nick's hand. "It doesn't matter,

Ellen. It's over. He's gone. I prefer to think of the happy memories we had and we did have some."

Nick squeezed her hand in return, a silent thank-you for her tact and diplomacy.

"I'm guessing that's yes." Ellen sighed and pressed her hands against her face. She stayed that way for a moment and Nick wondered if she was crying.

Finally she lowered her hands and gave them both a tremulous smile. "I want you—" she glanced at Bob who leaned forward and interrupted.

"We want you to know that in spite of our own grief we're happy for you two and we give you our blessing." Bob gave them a careful smile and Nick felt his muscles relax as if he'd been holding on to a heavy weight that he could finally drop.

"I'm thankful for you, Nick," Ellen added. "You've been a blessing in many ways to this family. And if it's okay with you, I'd like to pray together."

Nick tucked Beth's hand in his and before he lowered his head he gave her a quick smile. Her answering smile was radiant.

Then she looked down as Ellen began.

"Thank You, Lord for this young couple. We pray that You will bless their relationship. We pray that You will watch over them and help them through the pain that they've had to deal with. We pray You will continue to help us heal and we pray we may always see Your hand in our lives. Amen."

Nick kept his head down a moment longer, as a feeling of deep and utter peace caught him. He held on to the moment, thankful for what had happened to him. Thankful that he'd been brought into this family.

Then a cry from the bedroom upstairs snagged their attention. Kyle was awake.

Beth made a move to get up, but Nick stopped her. "I'll get him," he said.

"You don't mind?" Beth asked, hovering on the edge of the couch in case he changed his mind.

"No. I don't. After all, I did promise Jim that I would not only take care of you, but I would take care of his baby. And I still intend to keep those promises."

He got up and walked to Kyle's room, then pushed open the door. Kyle lay on his back, his arms thrashing, his wails filling the room. Nick scooped him up in his arms, holding the tiny body close as slowly Kyle's sobs eased. Nick shushed him, rocking him, his eyes closed as he inhaled the baby scent of this little boy. Beth's boy.

Our son. The thought lingered, filling his heart

with a joy he hadn't known he would ever experience. A noise at the door drew his attention. Beth stood there, one hand on the doorjamb, the other on her chest as if holding on to her heart.

"That looks good," she said quietly, walking toward them, her eyes shining with a happiness Nick had never seen before.

"Feels good," Nick said, rubbing his cheek over Kyle's downy-soft hair.

Beth stood alongside him. With his free arm Nick drew her close. "I love you so much," he said, brushing a kiss over her cheek, his feelings for her washing away the pain and guilt of the past.

Beth wrapped her arms around him and Kyle, closing the circle. "I love you, too." She laid her head on his shoulder and together they looked down at Kyle. Their son. The promise of a new beginning.

Epilogue

"So you think I should use these chipboard letters, or go with rub-ons on this card?"

Beth walked over to Angela, one of the participants in her card-making workshop, and looked over what she was doing.

"I'd go with the letters. I think it will give the card a little more dimension."

"I think you're right. Thanks." As Angela got up to get her supplies, Beth glanced at Kyle, sitting in his bouncy chair on one of the tables pushed together for the workshop.

"He is getting so big," Angela said, tickling his little feet.

Kyle waved his arms, blowing out bubbles of spit, expressing his joy with his life.

Trina, Beth's business partner, strolled into the back area of the store, a pencil tucked behind her ear, and a frown on her face as she stared at a piece of paper she held. After her confrontation with Nick, Shellie and her mother moved to Calgary. They put the store up for sale and Beth and Trina bought Crafty Corners.

"Have you had a chance to look at this?" She laid the paper on the table. "I don't think we ordered enough glimmer mist."

Beth glanced at the invoice. "I must have filled it out wrong. I'm sure I ordered two dozen bottles of the pearl and one dozen of the ruby."

Trina shrugged. "I thought so. Not a problem— I'll take care of it right away. If you have a chance, we really need to work on the website. I got some new stock in and I want to feature it on the first page."

"I think I might be able to work on it next week," Beth said. "I also have that new teaching video we need to upload."

Trina nodded her acknowledgment as the tinkling of the bell from the front door announced another customer.

Beth glanced through the doorway of the workroom and smiled. Nick stood in the middle of the store, glancing around. His cowboy hat was tipped back on his head, his jean jacket open, revealing a clean shirt instead of the stained T-shirt he'd had on this morning. He must have just come from the bank.

"Can I help you?" Beth asked with a teasing grin, walking up to him. "We've got some lovely new alcohol inks in as well as a new line of paper for summer that I'm sure you would love to use on your next project."

Nick pulled her close and dropped a kiss on her forehead in answer. Then he pulled back and stroked her hair back from her face. "I'm thinking my next project should be some kind of scrapbook," he grinned, playing along.

"For a special occasion?"

Nick adjusted his hat on his head and flashed her a grin. "Yeah. I'm going to buy in on a ranch and I wanted to document that."

Beth stared at him, squealed, then threw her arms around him. "You were approved for the loan for the ranch?"

"You're looking at Bob Carruthers's new partner." Nick lifted her off the floor in a bear hug, then set her down. He shot a frown at the group of ladies who had gathered in the doorway, watching them.

"Ladies, this is my husband, Nick Colter," Beth said, still holding on to Nick. "Nick, these are the members of my latest card-making class."

Nick tipped his hat and one of the ladies sighed, her hand resting on her chest.

Nick turned to Beth. "I thought I could pick up Kyle. Ellen said she'd watch him this afternoon. She knew you'd be busy at the shop."

"I'll get his stuff together," Beth said.

Beth went to the bathroom in the back of the store and grabbed Kyle's diaper bag, checking to make sure everything was inside. "I've got the car seat in my car," she said as she walked into the room. "So you'll either have to move it or take my car…." Her words trailed off to be replaced by a smile.

Nick was holding Kyle in one arm, nodding as Inelda, one of the women taking Beth's class, chatted with him.

"Your wife has the best ideas," Inelda said. "I'm so glad she took over this store. The products they carry and the classes have opened a whole new world for me. I can hardly wait for the next class. She's going to be showing us how to use a Cricut to make a diorama. Very exciting."

Nick just nodded and Beth was surprised his eyes didn't glaze over. She knew he was proud of her venture—taking over Crafty Corners in partnership with Trina—but he got lost when she delved too far into the intricacies of die-cut

The Baby Promise

machines, paper patterns and which ink was the best for stamping.

"I've got Kyle's bag," she said, raising her voice so he could hear her above the chatter of the women working around the table.

Nick spun around and strode toward her, smiling his relief. He bent over to kiss her and Beth could hear a few sighs around the room.

"By the way, Nick, your baby is adorable," Angela said. "I think he looks just like you."

Nick gave Beth a wink. "I should be so lucky to be so good-looking," he said, not bothering to correct Angela. "I'll be waiting for you at home," he said to Beth. "And tonight I'll make supper."

"Is that a promise?" Beth asked.

"It is, my dear," he said with a grin. Then he walked out of the store, a dozen pairs of eyes watching his progress.

"Will he really make supper?" Angela asked, her tone incredulous.

"It doesn't happen very often, but if Nick promises he will do it, it'll get done." Beth smiled. "Nick always keeps his promises."

* * * * *

Dear Reader,

As I wrote this story, I struggled with a couple of things. One was that I don't know what it is like to be a soldier or the wife of a soldier. I knew that whatever I wrote would be a pale copy of what many of our troops and their families deal with. But at the same time, I do feel that we, as North Americans living in a free country, can understand and appreciate the sacrifices that our troops make to keep this world free and to give people in other countries a taste of the many freedoms we so often take for granted.

I want to thank our soldiers and their families for their sacrifices and for their heroism. Ultimately, I pray for peace in the world and that until that happens we may know that the God of all ages and all places holds us in His loving and faithful hands.

Carolyne Aarsen

QUESTIONS FOR DISCUSSION

1. What was your first impression of Beth Carruthers? Did you sense a secret in her?

2. How would you feel if you were in Beth's place—a single mother recently widowed?

3. Nick was initially reluctant to stay at the ranch and keep his friend's promise. Discuss some of the reasons he might have felt that way.

4. What was your reaction to Nick's feelings of guilt? Why do you think he felt that way?

5. Do you personally know any soldiers who have come home from overseas? What were some of their reactions to coming home?

6. Beth's family seemed distant from her, and yet at the same time they seemed to love her. How do you think they might have contributed to Beth choosing Jim as a husband?

7. What are your feelings about Beth and Jim's relationship? Beth had times when she regretted marrying Jim. Have you ever made major

life decisions you regretted? How did you deal with them?

8. Beth said she would never chase after a man again. Why would she have said that?

9. What do you think Beth's card-making said about her? What do you think she was trying to do with her craft?

10. What was your reaction to Beth's relationship with her in-laws? What could she have done differently?

11. What was the theme of the book? What was the author trying to say about promises?

LARGER-PRINT BOOKS!

GET 2 FREE LARGER-PRINT NOVELS PLUS 2 FREE MYSTERY GIFTS

Love Inspired

Larger-print novels are now available...

LILP10R

Love Inspired®

SUSPENSE

RIVETING INSPIRATIONAL ROMANCE

Watch for our new series of
edge-of-your-seat suspense novels.
These contemporary tales
of intrigue and romance
feature Christian characters
facing challenges to their faith...
and their lives!

NOW AVAILABLE IN REGULAR
& LARGER-PRINT FORMATS

Steeple
Hill®

Visit:
www.SteepleHill.com

LISUSDIR10